THE SECRET SISTER

Fotini Tsalikoglou

THE SECRET SISTER

*Translated from the Modern Greek
by Mary Kitroeff*

Europa
editions

Europa Editions
214 West 29th Street
New York, N.Y. 10001
www.europaeditions.com
info@europaeditions.com

Copyright © 2013 by Fotini Tsalikoglou, Kastaniotis Editions S.A. Athens
First Publication 2015 by Europa Editions

Translation by Mary Kitroeff
Original title: 8 ώρες 35 λεᾷτά
Translation copyright © 2015 by Europa Editions

Library of Congress Cataloging in Publication Data is available
ISBN 978-1-60945-245-2

Tsalikoglou, Fotini
The Secret Sister

Book design by Emanuele Ragnisco
www.mekkanografici.com

Prepress by Grafica Punto Print – Rome

Printed in the USA

For Constantinos,
again and always

I didn't go to the moon, I went much further—
for time is the greatest distance between two places.
—TENNESSEE WILLIAMS,
The Glass Menagerie

CONTENTS

THE SECRET SISTER

Eight hours and thirty-five minutes. And then? Where will I end up, Amalia? In a place our mother was afraid to love; and yet, that is where Menelaos was born, and that is where Erasmia and the other Frosso grew up. How can I end up alone in a foreign land? And why now, after all these years? An inscrutable and dark journey. At the most difficult moment. I'm afraid, Amalia. Sunday, January 20, 2013, eleven in the morning.

Just before takeoff. New York to Athens. Seat 3A, a window seat. The seat next to me is empty. It's you who's sitting in it, Amalia. No stranger will disturb you. You're strapped in now, just like me. On the screen, our trajectory. The flying beast—a little dot traveling across the sky. I'm sitting in its belly. And so are you. Why make this journey to a land she never sought out? She'd trick me with all kinds of ruses and hide the truth. She'd drag me off to museums. She'd show me pediments, funerary steles, *kouroi* and *korai* statues. "Look," she'd say to me, "open your eyes and look, or you'll be lost." I was seven years old. She'd lend me her eyes. But, at a certain point, it became clear—clear as day—that she was revolted by her country. She changed her name. Nothing reminiscent of Greece. Lale Andersen. The mutant mother.

"None of you are to call me Frosso ever again. From this day onwards, my name is Lale."

Every trip is a search for something. Aside from what you say, that which is evident, there's something more. Like a passionate and impossible love. Without it you're incomplete. A piece that's missing and makes you say: "Now is the time to find it." And yet, there couldn't be a more inopportune time for me to find anything in this country. Or not? Could it be that at the very moment this country is giving in to the unthinkable and everything seems to be collapsing—could it be that now is the right time? "Look or you'll be lost." How can I look if I don't take my body, my arms, my eyes, my mind over there? You're with me in my luggage, Amalia, together with a photograph, an empty notebook and a guidebook to Athens. It'll be my first time there. What am I looking for, who will tell me? A poet spent an entire afternoon searching for the other tiger, the one he needed to finish his poem. Otherwise he couldn't write.

"Don't think so much, Jonathan, you lose yourself in your thoughts, and I, I lose you," you used to tell me.

To lose myself and to love you, to lose myself so as to love you, Amalia. You're my soul! In a few moments, JFK will be far away, and the skyscrapers, the park, the quays, the river, the ocean will all become postcards, pictures from a paper amusement park, shimmering in the light of day until the sky swallows them up.

How will I survive being so far away?

* * *

"You're naked, you'll catch cold. Bundle up. Is that how you're coming to the park? It's December. Look at how warmly I'm dressed. Run and get your anorak."

Stop telling me what to do.

"See, now you have a nosebleed, you'll—"

Oh, but so do you, Amalia. Your nose is bleeding—you and me both.

"*Damn it, I got it all over my T-shirt! Jeeesus, look at this mess. A handkerchief, Jonathan! Tie it tightly round my arm.*"

A handkerchief?

"*It stops the bleeding. Grandma says so, remember? Anthoula, quickly, get a hankie. Come on, let's get a move on.*"

Anthoula, Grandma, we're going. If she asks, tell her we're in the park. We won't be long.

"*You poor thing, still hoping she'll ask . . . She doesn't give a damn . . . She's one messed up woman.*"

She's not a woman, Amalia! She's our mama!

"*She's still a woman.*"

Oh, just shut up!

With a handkerchief tied around each arm, we'd rush out onto 57th Street and arrive breathless at the park, the squirrels were never afraid of us, with blades of grass, roots, seeds and acorns we would win them over. Cheep-cheep, cheep-cheep, they knew the sound of our voices; they'd come out of their hiding places and scurry towards us, with an inexplicable and impermissible sense of trust.

"That's how everything should be," you'd say, taking out the acorns you'd hid in your pocket.

The last flight of Delta Air Lines. The service from New York to Athens is being discontinued. Is Greece not a viable destination? "Fasten your seat belts." In a few minutes, the lights will be dimmed for takeoff. A sudden lull before the explosion of deafening noises.

The lights were dimmed then too for takeoff. I remember the night. The initial darkness. That's where I came from. Like 6.92 billion others. Each one of them another. We all came out of the same darkness. From the nighttime of a womb. It was Sunday, seven o'clock in the morning. She cried out. Two or three loud screams. That was it. They gave her an epidural. She insisted on keeping her eyes open. I was born without anyone asking me. She wanted me to be born at home. Persistently she insisted.

"I want to give birth at home—not at the hospital."

Her parents, Grandpa Menelaos and Grandma Erasmia, were frightened.

"Frosso, that's crazy talk!"

"Let me do as I wish."

"Frosso, for God's sake! What are you thinking? You have a birth ahead of you, not a death. You're about to give birth and you act like a dying woman who insists on leaving her last breath in her home, so that her soul might rest in peace. Is it all the same to you—the first and last breath?"

"I'll do as I please."

"Are you confusing the new life that's struggling to come out into the light with one that's already on its way to darkness?"

Strange and weird Mama. "It's my birth," she'd say, "and it's my child, so I'll do as I please." I felt her vocal cords in my stomach . . . I was only two inches long and already I could hear her voice inside me. "I want him here, in my bed, I want the first thing he sees to be the light coming from the river." She didn't want me. She wanted to want. That was all.

It was summer, and the Hudson River poured golden reflections over the houses stretching along its shores. That was where our house was. At first—and for a few days to come—it was her place of residence. Her one and only place. But that didn't last long. There was no father.

I never knew my father. And neither did you, Amalia.

"Was it the same man?"

But we're the same. Look at how alike we are! Look, if you don't believe me, look in the mirror.

"Why, yes, we're the same, Jonathan, we're the same."

So perhaps we share the same father . . . what difference does it make? She needed a seed for her son. And another for her daughter. I was her son. Her first child. With you it was different, Amalia. For you maybe she also wanted a great love. Maybe not. You can't order great loves. They come and find you and, if you are not frightened off, they give you unbearable bliss.

"At home nobody ever spoke of these things. It was stifling, all the things they hid from us."

Sealed lips hid secrets. And if someone, Grandma, let's say, or Grandpa, or Anthoula, tried to speak, it would be like robbing a church. It was sacrilege for anyone to try and ask something about "Daddy" or "Amalia and Jonathan's daddy," or to imply something about "Mrs. Efrosyni Argyriou's husband." Who makes the rules? Who enforces them, and at what cost? Each family is fed by its secrets. Like a strangely bulimic climbing vine, the unrevealed secrets embrace the family's flesh a little tighter each day, until in the end they become one with it. You can't tell the vine from the flesh. A couple joined for all time, and if you try to pry it apart, you destroy it. Dust, damp, lichen and bugs erode the leafy, green body. In the summer, when the smell of something rotting won't let you be, you pray to God for a breath of fresh air.

* * *

An oppressive heat is coming out of the air conditioning—"Please, Miss, could you fix the ventilator?" The revolving nozzle above my head is adjusted and the temperature drops at once. I can't wait for takeoff. A couple of rows in front of me an elderly woman makes the sign of the cross. The moment just before becoming airborne is ideal for entreaties. Up there in the sky, in a few moments, our fate will lie in God's hands. If you grow up without a father, you dream of those hands—sometimes gently healing your wounds, and other times mean and merciless, choking the life out of you.

"Heavens above, Frosso, one doesn't play with God!"

Our mother played with him. She borrowed his omnipotence and his arbitrariness. She answered to no one. To give birth to her son in her bedroom, to cut the umbilical cord herself, to wash off the blood, to spend the day with the newborn in her arms, defying the rules of physical and mental health—she would do all these things and more. To reveal to no one who her son's father was. And, two years later, to be pregnant with a daughter, whose father was unknown once again. To give her children names like Jonathan and Amalia for her own indecipherable reasons. I assume she liked the sound of "Jonathan"—there's an extended musicality to it, at "Jo-" the tongue goes up as if it's singing, and then at "-nathan" it settles down again, a little sadly. As for "Amalia," maybe it was the first syllable, "Am-," that sounds like the French for soul. I'll never know.

You have to be pretty unhappy to always want to do things your way. Grandma, Grandpa, Anthoula, Stamatis, our Greek friends, Grandpa's colleagues, Peter, Matthew, John—none of them dared contradict her. Were they frightened of her misery? And when she started drinking like a fish, and there'd be no trace of her for hours, even days, again no one said anything. And when her belly began to grow, again no one asked about the whys and the wherefores. What else did they fear besides her misery? God punishes those who stand in the way of the insane desires of insanely miserable people. Who doesn't want God's grace? And if you're guilty, you might want it even more . . .

Were all of them guilty? Why? How long did we live in ignorance? And could it be that when the secret is revealed, when the darkness is lifted, then you find yourself in another delusion?

You lean over and whisper something in my ear, the roar of the plane's engine grows louder, I try to make out your words.

"*Jonathan,*" you say, "*what you will never know will always be stronger, don't kid yourself, do you want me to tell you what you accomplish every time you think you understand?*"

Yes, tell me.

"*A meatless bone of truth is what you're holding in your hand, and you're licking it and saying 'this tastes good'.*"

Don't stop talking to me, Amalia.

The voice is lost, all I catch is the word "crumbs" and the phrase "the bones of truth." The noise drowns out the rest.

The engines sound like something just before an explosion. The elderly woman is still praying.

What would she think if I suddenly went up to her and said: "It's no use, my dear lady, however many signs of the cross you make, nothing will change. The sky is self-sufficient; a cloudless flight does not obey entreaties."

Instead of screaming to her face that "fear, Madam, is a prison, and in any case you can't exorcise it," I leave her in peace. My mind goes back again to my fearless mother.

At the last moment, certain complications put an end to her reckless plans. No doctor would take the risk of a home birth. And so I wasn't born at number 380 Riverside Drive, but at St. Luke's-Roosevelt Hospital on 59th Street. Shortly after I left her insides to come out into the light, she wrapped me up in a blanket as dainty as lace and, hardly giving them time to cut the umbilical cord and wash off the blood, she rushed me home. She almost kidnapped me. The chauffeur was waiting in the courtyard. "Hurry, we're late!" she shouted at him. It was Sunday. It took us only twenty minutes to get from Midtown Manhattan to the Upper West Side. Our house anxiously awaited my arrival. The silk sheets on her bed, the soap, the smell of cleanliness, sandalwood and lemon. Outside there was the smell of the river. On the first night of my life I slept without fear, she never left my side, her breast had milk, plenty of milk, it's as if I can still taste its tartness on my tongue. There are times when I despise milk and all dairy, big avenues and long journeys. There are times when I hate orphan boys and their bitches of mothers, their missing fathers and this entire city. There are times when I can't stand a city that never sleeps. The Big Apple. Its incessant hum which, if you let your guard down, will hypnotize you and then good luck finding yourself again, among the crowds moving along the streets like a river, amid the aroma of exotic foods and charred meat in the streets, amid the museums and the cathedrals. And yet, this is my city. This is where I was born. This is where I learned to love you, Amalia, the long river and the ocean. The skyscrapers made me woozy. I'd avoid looking up at them. Is the only way to avoid constant motion sickness to become an ocean yourself?

The sky is strongly reminiscent of the sea. We're flying at thirty-six thousand feet. Why this sudden journey? It only took me a minute to decide on it. I left in a hurry. Like a burglar who disappears when he hears suspicious noise and leaves the loot behind so he won't get arrested. I left to get away.

I left in the middle of everything. My whole life. As if that too had been stolen. Like someone who's been guilty for a long time, I dreaded being locked up. Is the Argyriou family to blame for all this, Amalia? Our family? Is that who makes me feel like a thief? Makes me want to save myself? Hush, don't say anything, don't say "all families are like that."

"And yet, Jonathan, it's true. No one can be saved from their family."

In a few hours I had my tickets and my luggage ready. I, who hate moving around; I, who, if I had the straps, would tie myself down to the bed at night, in case, like a sleepwalker, I get up and disappear; I, who, if I could, would keep myself like a heavy statue on solid ground—here I am now strapped in an airplane seat, preparing for the sudden turbulence of a transatlantic flight. I left everything behind and got up and left.

"There was no other way, Jonathan. You know that."

The lights will go out, are going out, have gone out. The engines are growling. The monster is rising up into the sky. In its belly, I sit dreaming. The noise drives me crazy, like a bomb ready to explode inside me, I cover my ears. Unexpectedly, the face of a madman enters my head. Who can control the mind's workings? December 1993. Our respectable Catholic school has organized a Christmas party at the Blue Mountain charity. Do you remember, Amalia? "Sensitization visits" they called them, to the indigent homeless. The foundation had its own history. It was set up with money donated by the Rockefeller family, in memory of one of their sons who had died on a trip to New Guinea, a horrible death though the exact circumstances were unknown.

The airplane has taken off. A smiling young woman with golden tiger eyes is serving fruit juice; I'm in Business Class, I paid a pretty penny for this trip.

Horrible deaths sometimes lie behind donations and charitable foundations. I didn't want to go to Blue Mountain. I had a bad feeling that day. I held my school bag tightly to my chest, as if carrying it to my side would cause all the misfortunes in the world to rain down on me. Walking beside me, without a care in the world, you were humming a tune. We all had the same plaid schoolbags; our school was ordered and respectable. It was Christmas and all we disciplined pupils, like the Magi bearing gifts, were to offer food and money to the most destitute of people. But for some reason, I didn't want to be there. *Let's go somewhere else, Amalia, come on, let's go while there's still time. Let's go to the docks, let's go down to Battery Park, let's get on a boat, let's take the Staten Island ferry, let's soak up some rays, let's see how the Statue of Liberty looks from the water. Let's get out of here, Amalia.* I didn't tell you anything. We stayed at the party. The residents of the shelter all stood together, wearing clean clothes and hesitant smiles, looking at us as awkwardly as we looked at them. We offered them the food and sweets. Our teacher gave them an envelope with nine hundred dollars. "God bless you," came to our ears from every corner and then we all sang: "*Have a holly, jolly Christmas; / It's the best time of the year . . . / . . . And when you walk down the street / Say hello to friends you know / And everyone you meet.*" Your voice stood out. Your divine voice, as Grandma used to say. And so the party was about to come to an end in such a lovely way, compassionately, generously, with a pleasant tune coming from the record player and the day gloriously ending. A sense of relief. Nothing bad had happened. I had been wrong to worry. That tightness in my chest had gone—and then it happened.

A dark-skinned man, in his fifties, with a crazed look, a tense smile and rotten teeth, came up to me and, before anyone could restrain him, he grabbed my wrist with the strength of a prehistoric animal and held my hand captive in his own. I tried to pull away, terrified and repulsed, trying to take back my stolen hand, and then he whispered, but loud enough to be heard by everyone, and certainly by Amalia: "Son, you, you, my son, you are my boy." I was struggling with the beast, I don't know for how long. At some point I freed my hand. My plaid schoolbag fell to the ground. "Time to go," said Miss Jones. She said it blithely, as if nothing had happened or in order to pretend nothing had happened. My heart was a lump of dry earth, one breath and it would fall apart. I bent down and picked up my bag, I held it tightly as if it was my earthen heart. And then Christopher my schoolmate's voice was heard:

"Ma'am, that dark gentleman, that man who grabbed Jonathan, did you notice, ma'am, that he looked just like Jonathan, that he was his spitting image?"

And nobody spoke, except for you, Amalia, your eyes spoke and said:

"Are you crazy? That's nonsense. That madman looked nothing like my brother!"

"Yes, that's exactly what I had said then, Jonathan. It was a lie."

And then the visit was over. You stayed on at school for your music class and I went home alone. They were waiting for me and the table was set. It was dinnertime. I sat down in my seat, and when they asked me "What happened in school today?" I replied, "I met my father. I saw him today for the first time."

Menelaos was thunderstruck, Grandma went to the kitchen to get some water, and Mama kept on eating her meal: roasted lamb with potatoes. Then Anthoula brought peeled oranges that smelled of cinnamon and spearmint.

"Open your mouth, sweet child. Eat. Oranges are full of power and health."

I was keeping my mouth obstinately shut. When my sister isn't here, what do I need power and health for? I want her to be here, to play the piano. To sing "The Northern Star" again. Have you ever heard such a beautiful voice? It's like the song of the mermaids.

"You're exaggerating, Jonathan. If that were the case, then I'd . . ."

Be quiet.

* * *

The airplane is now flying at thirty thousand feet.

"What would you like to drink?" the flight attendant asks me solicitously.

When you grow up without a father, you make others want to take care of you. They might even think more highly of you. They sense you're emitting an invisible fortitude, as if you've taken on the strength of the absent one.

"It's the blood talking," said Anthoula one day while you were singing. What did she mean?

Amalia, what does "It's the blood talking" mean?

"Why are you asking me? You should have asked others, back then."

There's no time. People die, and you have to make sure you learn, while they're alive, all the unintelligible words they've uttered, the allusive remarks, the censored thoughts. There's no time. You have to make sure you clear up the shadows before they swallow you up and then you turn into a shadow-man, like so many others. Anthoula's gone,

Grandpa, Grandma, they're all gone. I never found out what she meant by: "It's the blood talking."

"That's why people travel, Jonathan."

What do you mean, Amalia?

"That sometimes we come home to learn about all these things, before—"

Go on, why did you stop?

"Jonathan, the journey is yours."

You're with me.

"You're traveling to Greece alone."

You're with me.

"Alone. Don't kid yourself. How could I be with you? Are you forgetting, or are you pretending to forget?"

Be quiet.

A humming noise . . . The sky, an ocean that gives out no light, and a quilt of dark clouds inviting us to unfamiliar and therefore dangerous dreams. Sixty-four minutes have passed and still no turbulence. "Captain Watson and his crew would like to welcome you onboard . . . " A man across the aisle wedges a pillow under his head and prepares to sleep. "The duration of our flight is eight hours and thirty-five minutes. Expected time of arrival in Athens is 9 o'clock local time . . . " My fellow traveler hasn't touched his tray of juice, nuts and snacks. Satiated business class passengers,

Menelaos Argyriou was never one of you. His family lived with hunger, but never feared it. They grew attached to their homeland, perhaps because from the very start they missed it, it was never a given, it never gave them a sense of safety and security. They traveled far away with their minds focused on the wound. They never felt closer to their homeland than when they were far away.

We were born and raised "far away."

"*I know, Jonathan. New York, our city, never hurt us. Never frightened us. How lucky we were, Jonathan, to have grown up here and not over there.*"

"Over there" was a dot on the map. Green and dark grey and blue. In the Eastern Mediterranean, at the southernmost tip of the Balkan Peninsula, with seas and thousands of islands, with a dry and rocky soil, with foreign-sounding mountains, lakes and rivers—Olympus, Smolikas, Voras, Tymphi, Vardousia, Volvi, Vegoritida, Kerkini, Strymonas, Arachthos, Alfios.

The soft blanket is wrapped around the body of my unknown fellow traveler, who is now preparing to sink into a luxurious sleep. What does he have in common with Menelaos Argyriou? Wrapped in a filthy blanket covered in lice and vomit, on the ship's third class deck, he sailed to

America to start the story of a new life from the beginning. It was the second time. He was now leaving behind more things that he would have to pretend to forget. Not only his land and orchard, but Little Frosso with her unworn red dress. Little Frosso never made it to America. Her journey was interrupted halfway there, on the seventh day. Her body arched, bent over and sank. She never made it here and so it was as if she never left there.

"From the time we were born, inside us we have confused here with there, now with then, before with after."

Our family walked a tightrope between oblivion and truth. That's how we grew up. Like so many other families since the beginning of time, the things it had to forget were more than those it could bear to remember.

"Years later, when she chose her new name, the name Frosso was banned. And along with it the word 'Greece'."

Her eyes stopped looking at us.

"Her breath smelled bad when she came near me. I wanted to run away."

Her voice broke.

"You wake up in the morning and the whole world has changed."

She would get angry at anyone who called her Frosso. Tipsy from drinking, more and more every day.

"And you, Jonathan, struggling to make heads or tails of it all. Even just a little bit. Otherwise you can't live. But the heads might bite and the tails might sting."

In eight hours, everything will be different. I'll begin to understand everything that escapes me now.

"Trapped in a dream. But if you don't take a risk, how will you be saved?"

On the Holy Rock of the Acropolis—in a few hours I'll be there. As I look at the amber color of the Marbles, will I be able to see your eyes? Or will I just hear your voice whispering once more: "You're alone here, a stranger in a strange land"?

"There are altars there and sanctuaries that aren't visible, and underground arcades that lead to the sea. You'll put on a clean white shirt, Jonathan, and if there's a southern wind blowing, you'll hear the sound of the waves."[1]

---

[1] An allusion to Freud's visit to the Acropolis in September 1903. He had worn a clean white shirt and, in a letter to Martha Freud, he had written: "They say that the amber color of the columns at twilight is the most beautiful thing in the world."

The young woman with the khaki-colored pumps is getting ready to serve lunch.

"Later," I tell her.

She flashes a smile at me and turns to the other passengers.

* * *

Sometimes Mama's face would glow. On certain Friday afternoons, when she would come by the school to pick me up and take me to the Metropolitan Museum's gallery to see the statues. I was just a kid, but she would make me look at them for hours. What was I supposed to make of them? "Just look at them, that's enough," she would say. She seemed happy then. Was I her favorite son or something else? I saw statues, marbles and nude men, and young women, pots and talismans, jewelry, clasps and necklaces— what was I supposed to make of them? The museum guards, the doormen, the guides, they all knew her. "Hello, Ma'am." "This is my son." Why did she want me with her? She definitely went there alone. Perhaps even every day. At five thirty the Met closed. We were always the last ones to leave. One day, she led me in front of a marble stele. It showed a woman next to a man. The man was naked, one hand resting on his chin, the other holding a sword, looking at the woman. She was facing away from him. She was wrapped in a piece of fabric that enveloped her body in folds. Between them stood an ewer. "It's a lekythos," she said, and then: "Write it down." In my notebook I wrote down "lekythos" in my child's handwriting. I was seven years old, for God's sake, what sense could I make of a funerary stele? They were both dead. The man was a warrior, he was off to battle; the woman would make a libation, she would sacrifice to the gods. On the wall hung a soldier's uniform, a helmet and a sword. The battle would prove deadly. The man would be killed. The woman would die of persistent and protracted sorrow. "Write it down," she said, "write down that the woman died." Next to the word "lekythos," I jotted down the verb "died."

Amalia?

"Yes, Jonathan?"

I wish you could have been with me on those Friday afternoons.

"That wasn't possible, Jonathan, I had my piano lessons and my singing. Friday was my music day, have you forgotten?"

Have you any idea how often I hear your voice filling me up inside, like a benevolent sea, like . . . I haven't the words to say sea, sun, son, song . . . Do you remember your voice, Amalia?

"I remember, Jonathan. Your voice is the last thing of yours you forget."

The Northern Star
Will bring clear skies
But before a sail appears in the sea
I'll turn into a wave and fire
To embrace you, foreign land . . .

Stop, Amalia! It makes me want to cry.
"There's no point in that. Just listen to the voice."

And you, lost motherland of mine, so far away
You'll become a caress and a wound
When day breaks in another land . . .

When you cry in flight, the flight attendant comes to see to you.

"Excuse me, sir, is anything wrong? Can I help you?"

"It's nothing, I'll be okay. I just had a curious dream. I'll be fine in a minute."

Now I'm flying to life's celebration
Now I'm flying to the feast of my joy

My olden moons
My newfound birds
Chase away the sun and daylight from the hill
And watch me go by
Like lightning across the sky.[2]

When she went to City Hall to change her name, our visits to the museum abruptly stopped. My notebook disappeared. When I searched, it was nowhere to be found. This woman is our mother. I was born and raised in New York. I never knew my father's name, never saw his face. Two years after me, my sister was born. I don't know who her father is or if we have the same father. Our mother doesn't tell us truths. She tells

[2] "The Northern Star" is a popular song written in 1963 by Manos Hadjidakis to lyrics by the poet Nikos Gatsos.

us lies, and even more than the lies are the things that are lost in silence.

The flight attendant is young and pretty. I remember those Fridays, when she too was transformed into an unexpectedly beautiful creature. Attractive? Yes, you could go so far as to call her attractive. There are times when you mistake her for a young woman, but she's well past fifty. The others died years ago. The three of us live in a big apartment.

"'The three of us' did you say, Jonathan? Are we back to that again? You said 'The three of us live.'"

I will not respond to that, Amalia. I'll go on. She drinks incessantly. The empty bottles of cranberry and apple juice, vodka and whiskey.

"Disheveled and unkempt, she wanders around like a shadow of her shadow."

In her own little world, like we don't even exist.

"Looking for tenderness in the void."

She wasn't always like this. Do you remember her, Amalia? Do you remember her when she wasn't like this? Nicely dressed, with freshly shampooed hair, brightly colored scarves around her neck and an elegant fur hand muff for the winter cold. You never said so, but you were afraid you'd take after her.

"Yes, I didn't want to take after her. In anything. I didn't want to have her voice. I was in the bathroom, singing, the door was closed, Anthoula got confused. 'What a beautiful song, Mrs. Frosso! Don't stop!' 'No, Anthoula, it's me.'"

Amalia, that woman has nothing of yours. You run and hide when you hear her coming back at night, at some ungodly hour, walking slowly up the stairs and you lock yourself up in your room, afraid to see yourself in that damaged face. Sweetheart, you have nothing of hers; it's all yours, the eyes, the smell, your skin; you have nothing of hers.

"Her voice, Jonathan, is the same as mine. It's been years. She was in her room and I heard her humming a song. The door was ajar. I slipped inside. She didn't notice. 'The south wind came, the north wind came, the waves they came to take you / My love, you flew away from me / Because you were the sky.' I got goose bumps. 'Mama, what a beautiful song! Mama, sing some more!' She stopped suddenly. 'Don't come in like that, without knocking, into someone else's room.' I don't want to be like her, Jonathan."

She was born in Astoria, Queens. We were born in Manhattan. Years went by. Grandpa died. Grandma moved to an old folks' home. It was her own decision. You would never do something so heartless. Nor would you ever let Anthoula leave the house and disappear into the crowds of Manhattan. And if it were up to you, you would never let me travel alone, especially now, to that country that's sinking. How can I get rid of dreams and age-old darknesses, how can I turn myself into something I have not yet become, in order to make room enough inside me for this unknown land?

Should I think of the other Frosso, with her twenty-year-old body, before history broke her in pieces? Should I think of her vegetable garden in Podarades, her garden, the pit that's only for flowers and not for the buried bodies of friends, relatives who once came together and are now like strangers and like hate? Should I conjure up before me a girl who didn't want to leave that place which later everyone would want to leave? Shall I meet Little Frosso of New Ionia and Cappadocia? Should I listen to her song? The color of her voice? And then should I not be afraid, should I hear the sound her body made as it dove into the deep?

The iron bird lurched as if rudderless. The sign just went on: "Fasten seat belt."

* * *

"Don't be afraid of anyone," Grandma Erasmia used to tell us when bedtime came around. Then we'd say our prayers. They were made of two parts. Two halves. Half English, half Greek. "Dear God, please take good care of our family, *Iesous Christos nikai ke ola ta kaka skorpai*, and there is no evil on earth."

It was the winter of 1995, Sunday lunchtime. Grandpa was ill in the hospital. That day, Grandma left him for a little and came home. Mama was out. "I want to talk to you," she said. "There's a story I want you to hear." Do you remember, Amalia? We were unprepared. What we saw, that was all we knew, and the things that couldn't be seen were as if nonexistent. "I had a sister," said Grandma. We gave each other a puzzled look. She had a sister, and why did she only tell us now, why did she let all these years go by? "Here she is," she said, "I have her right here," and she took the picture out of her bosom. "She was your Grandpa's first wife," she said, "*my little sister*." Her little sister looked at us with bleary, timeworn eyes, her hair wavy, her beautiful hair, her nose, her cheeks, the line of her chin, her dimple, deeper on the right, and the suspicion of a smile. *"This is my sister."* Here, I carry that little photo with me now. Here, I have it. That tired photo. So Grandma had a sister and this sister whom she was revealing to us now for the first time was Grandpa's first wife? You had Bellino in your arms. You put him down and went to her side.

"Bellino was in no mood for petting that day."

You sat next to her. You loved her, I knew it from the beginning, more than you did our mother or me; it was her, Erasmia, whom you loved. Did you know the story? Did you pity her situation? How safe an indicator of love is pity? You took the yellowed Frosso in your fingers, you stood looking at her for a long time, and the whole time Grandma was speaking, you held her paper dead sister in your hands. Why didn't we think it strange, Amalia? Why didn't we say: "Why haven't you told us of your sister all this time? Why now?"

"It was so beautiful, Jonathan, the photo!"

Did we already know? How many things do children know without knowing? Grandma began talking to us slowly and steadily at first and then without pausing, in a haste that would not let up, in a single breath.

"She was five years old and I was seven, I held her by the hand, September of '22,[3] frantic, we were running along the quay at Smyrna, in one minute we had to leave, we had to abandon our identity, in one minute what we were had ceased to exist, tightly, as tightly as possible, I held her by the hand so as not to lose her, my little sister, everything was getting lost then, there was nothing easier than to get lost, I don't remember anything else, only the cries, the weeping of the women who were losing their children, babies screaming because their mothers had left them to save themselves, dark instincts transform you at such times, I saw a mother tearing her son from her arms and setting him on the ground, so she would be lighter and able to save herself, and another cutting her finger, so as to be the same as her injured child which was screeching as if it were being slaughtered by a thousand swords, and she was howling in the same way as her child, they say that you

[3] Smyrna was a cosmopolitan city with a large Greek population. Its destruction by the Turkish army in 1922 and the forced population exchanges that followed between Greece and Turkey marked the end of the continuous presence of Greeks in Asia Minor for 3,000 years. Seven-year-old Erasmia and her five-year-old sister were among the 1.5 million refugees who managed to flee to Greece.

can't die another's death, but I saw mothers dying
their children's deaths, I saw the Turks, the charg-
ing horses, the dust, the dogs barking fiercely, a
roar, dead bodies strewn about like they were nothing, people running like a river to the sea, we were
carried off by the raging torrent of the crowd, from
Talas,[4] that's all I know, one name, Talas, and the
caves, the Fairy Caves they called them, pyramids
sculpted out of the rocks, near Goreme, that's
where we would play, my sister, who had the voice
of an angel, and I, that's what I remember, butter-
flies, the sound of an oud, a hill covered in orange
trees, and a mother, a father, relatives next to us,
cattle, horses, dogs, donkeys, us running to the
sea, they pushed us onto a rowboat, they were all
lost, my mother, Amalia, I never saw her again, nor
anyone else, I remember her voice, when foreign
hands grabbed her, 'my Little Frosso, the apple of
my eye, keep an eye out for her,' and then my eyes
grew dark, somebody pushed us onto a rowboat, I
shut my eyes, but I was holding onto her tightly, I
wasn't going to let her go, not for anything. They

[4] In the early 20th century, Talas, a town in Cappadocia, Asia Minor,
was home to 2,500 families, of which 1,000 were Christian Orthodox,
800 were Muslim and 700 were Armenian.

could have given me the sky and the earth below, and I would not have let go. With the ribbon I pulled off my plaits, I tied her hand tightly to mine. My Little Frosso, it's the two of us now, no more Fairy Caves, no more *hatırı* and *ciğer*, no more *hediye*, no more *canım*.[5] Gone is your voice that enchanted one and all. Little Frosso has the voice of an angel, she's a tiny little thing but you can be proud of her, and whoever picked up an oud and touched its chords, you'd start to sing: '*What do you care / Where I'm from / Whether from Karadassi / Or from Kordelio . . .* ' From the rowboat to a ship and from there from port to port until we arrived at a foreign harbor, Piraeus. We didn't say a word, we kept our mouths obstinately shut, as if someone wanted to force feed us something unbearable, we didn't make a sound, we just held each other tightly by the hand, I don't know for how many days . . . and then we ended up there. In this new land. 'It'll be like a homeland here,' they told us. The word 'like' made all the difference. But we grew up, we went to school, in New Ionia,[6] in

---

[5] *Hatırı*, "favor," *ciğer*, "heart," *hediye*, "gift," *canım*, "my soul."

[6] New Ionia is a suburb of Athens settled by Greek refugees from Asia Minor.

Podarades. We built a small life. A brother of Mama's helped us. That was it. We never spoke of other places, or of those who were lost. I held her tightly by the hand until she became a big girl. Up until the day Menelaos and Uncle came and told us:

"'We have good news: Frosso is going to marry well, Mr. Menelaos Argyriou, a young man, kind and hardworking, and with connections in America, you're both very lucky, who knows, Erasmia, perhaps fortune will smile on you too. Do you want to, Little Frosso, *do you want to*?'

"'Little Frosso nodded, said nothing, just nodded and looked me in the eye.

"'And you? And you, Erasmia, do you want to?'

"'But do you need to ask!' I said to her. 'What luck!' and I ran outside so they wouldn't see my tears.

"In three days Menelaos came, in six days the wedding took place, in seven days they left for America. That night I was alone for the first time in eighteen years . . . I cried my eyes out and felt happiness for my sister. There was no way of knowing that two months later, on August 17, 1940, Menelaos would come back alone and in a suitcase he would bring back Frosso's red dress without Frosso. Soon the war would break out. Those who could leave would leave. The others would stay and make do. It would be impossible to endure this war and everything that came after it,[7] we became strangers among ourselves, brother killed brother, son killed father, eyes grew dark with fear and hate. We didn't recognize our homeland. Eighteen years after Smyrna, the fire would follow us. As soon as Menelaos returned alone, I threw my arms around him.

"'Take me,' I said, 'take me away from here.'

"But he had already made up his mind, that's why he had come back: to take me with him.

"'You'll marry me, Erasmia, you'll take me to be your husband, I can't live anymore without you two.'

"It was the first time I saw a face so deeply saddened and determined. I thought of Little Frosso. How would she feel? And I said that my sister would be happy, no doubt about it. I don't know if I was being irrational, but I said that her

[7] After the end of World War II and the four-year German Occupation, Greece became embroiled in a civil war between the communists and the government forces which lasted until 1949. The polarization created by this war is still very evident in Greek society.

body, in the depths of the ocean where it lay, would find the way to tell me, 'But yes, do you need to ask, sister? You'll say yes and you'll marry Menelaos, and you'll go with him where I wasn't able to go,' and then I thought about how the brine and the damp preserve bodies and protect them from malicious decomposition, and how, with her body intact, with her child's heart, with her wavy hair, all in one piece as I first laid eyes on her, my little sister would give her consent, 'Go ahead, Erasmia, you go in my place,' she would tell me again and she would be filled with joy at Menelaos's proposal that I become his wife in her place. We each wanted what was best for the other. She wasn't destined to live, so I would do it for her, 'Keep an eye out for Little Frosso,' 'I'll keep an eye out for her.' Then I lost my nerve. I couldn't go through with it, I had to find more strength. I went to Saint Lucas, the priest was saying Mass. 'Lord, forgive me,' I said, it was the Archangel Michael in the icon, he smiled at me, 'Have a safe trip,' he said, 'Lord, forgive me,' I said again, and I got myself ready for the big journey.

"For two days in a row I saw the same dream, our mother in Goreme, in the Fairy Caves, 'Çok şükür yarabim sen biliyorsun,'[8] I began to cry, I couldn't understand what she was trying to say, I memorized the words, I went and found Agathi, the old woman who lived next door, who knew many things we knew nothing about.

"'What do those words mean?' I asked her.

"'Whose are they?'

"'My mother's.'

"'The dead one or the living one?' she asked me, and I thought it strange, because Agathi knew full well our mother wasn't living.

"'They're the dead one's words,' I said, 'I have no other.'

"'You do,' she said, 'you have another mother, she's the shadow of your dead sister, and she follows you around and gives you her blessing, and you'll carry with you one mother's shadow and the other mother's blessing and Godspeed to you.'

"That's what the old woman said, and I realized it was God's will and I ran to Menelaos, fell into his arms, 'I'm ready,' I said, and we went to the same church, Saint Lucas in Patissia, that's where we got married and the next day we held a memo-

[8] *Glory be to you, all-knowing God.*

rial service for Little Frosso, and the church was adorned with white roses and jasmine and daisies, which she loved, and they chanted 'He makes me lie down in green pastures,' and I cried inconsolably, but now everything was ready for us to leave. I hugged Menelaos, 'Let's go,' I said, 'we shouldn't be late,' I didn't want to stay in my country any longer, as if I could feel that soon war would break out and then the civil war with brothers like foreign bodies slaughtering each other, and erstwhile comrades betraying each other, 'Let's go, Menelaos, let's go,' and we boarded the big ship, for twenty-one days Menelaos held me tightly by the hand, he wouldn't let go of me for a moment and at night in the same bunk, and because he was a heavy sleeper, he kept me tied to his hand with a handkerchief. But I was in no danger, I didn't care about vomit, maggoty food, heavy seas, I was going to get to America no matter what. Everything seemed bearable to me. I had no intention of getting lost in the depths of the Atlantic. September 16, 1940. It was a Monday. It was foggy. The ship was called 'New Greece.' As it entered the harbor, we all came on deck. The doctors boarded to examine us. They carefully checked my eyes—the fundus was clear, there was no damage;

they examined my skin—I wasn't consumptive; my nails, my tongue, everything was clear. 'She's okay,' I was eligible to stay. We disembarked. A huge statue awaited us. 'It's the Statue of Liberty,' they told us. That's how we arrived here and struggled hard and became Grandpa Menelaos and Grandma Erasmia, and we did well, and then we brought Anthoula here, Agathi's cousin, to do the housework, and after twelve years your mother was born. And we named her Frosso."

She stopped talking then. I didn't dare look you in the eye, Amalia. What were you thinking that whole time?

"*Nothing, Jonathan. I was looking at Frosso's photo. How beautiful she was. That's all I could think about.*"

You said nothing, and neither did I. You went up to her, you reached out and stroked her hair. Suddenly she looked a thousand years old.

"I'm tired," Grandma said.

That was when you asked her: "Does Mama know? Does she know about Aunt Frosso, does she know about her name?"

You received no answer. Grandma got up with difficulty and lay down on the couch. Soon she'd fallen asleep.

"Soon she'd fallen asleep."

You were left looking at her. And I stood to the side and watched you, you were holding your breath in case you disturbed her sleep and then she'd feel uncomfortable about all the things she confided in us, all the indelicate and forbidden secrets. Did you know that was only the beginning? And that Erasmia's silver sleep held more secrets? How beautiful you were, Amalia! Dazzlingly beautiful. I had to close my eyes not to be blinded. When I opened them again I was a boy alone on a foreign continent, learning his history little by little.

"It was such a sunny day, Jonathan! The skyscrapers were bathed in light, whereas on overcast days they'd disappear into the clouds. It would soon be Halloween, Joanna and I were getting our costumes ready. I was going to dress up as a superstar, she was going to be a Himalayan cat, Michael was sweet on me, he had green eyes, Clarissa thought he was a dreamboat."

You were thirteen and I was fifteen. Michael was an idiot.

"The story ran on inside us. Children can endure all kinds of stories. They're saving their strength for what is to come."

Grandpa came back from the hospital sick.

"He never recovered. He dwindled with each passing day."

Grandpa died on the Thursday. On the Tuesday, two days earlier, I remember the day. It was right after school. You got a stain on the white velvet couch that was Grandma's prized possession and which was constantly in danger from unruly Bellino's nails. That day it had been left without its cover and as soon as you sat down it turned red. You became flustered. "Blood, I'm sorry," you stammered and ran to the bathroom. "I'm sorry, blood," I repeated, as if I'd just got my period with you, and I ran away in shame, as if trying to hide the sign of my secret gender. However, in two days' time I would be the only man in the house.

Grandpa died; he was eighty-one years old. The obituary in the *New York Times* read:

Menelaos Argyriou, aged 81, passed away on Thursday, February 8, 1996. He was born in Athens, Greece and he was a longtime resident of New York City. He is survived by his beloved wife Erasmia, born in Talas, Asia Minor, his daughter Lale Andersen and two grandchildren, Jonathan and Amalia.

We shall miss you, Menelaos.

*

Several friends showed up at the Memorial Park Funeral Home, old neighbors from Astoria, Grandpa's partner, the man who lived downstairs, the porter and his family, the chauffer, a lady from the convenience store. And then they all came to the house. Anthoula made savory pies with herbs, some more friends of Grandpa's came by, not many, an old neighbor from Astoria with his new wife and her kids, the lady from the ground floor and her dog. Bellino hid in the kitchen—he'd get restless around strangers,—Menelaos's partner and his two sons brought flowers and a big fish. That was it. A cousin called from Athens. I made the mistake of picking up the receiver.

"I'm his cousin, well, actually, I'm more like a brother, my name's Seraphim, you must have heard of me, sonny, my boy Sakis made it over to your parts a few months ago, but Menelaos never made it back here one last time, your poor grandfather, my boy, he needed to make it back here one more time, now that everything has changed, because last time he was very disappointed and Menelaos's heart didn't deserve to be so darkened, nobody deserves that, but him living in a foreign land all these years, he deserved better than that, because, you see . . . well . . . there was that accursed last time he came to see us, it was in the middle of the Dictatorship, in 1971,"[9] every few words his voice would break, "we went to our old haunt, down in Petralona, he was so glad to see me, so many years later, 'No matter how good it is over there, it's different here, even the bad stuff is different here,' he kept saying, over and over, and he began to sing a revolutionary song, but then everyone around us froze, and some even threatened us, 'We don't want any trouble here,' they said, so we got the hell out of there, and you know what? The people who kicked us out were our friends, our buddies, your grandfather was so upset, you can't imagine, he began to cry, 'I don't want a homeland like this,' he said, 'I'm better off over there, at the ends of the earth.' And he left with a heavy heart. If only you knew how ashamed I felt! And then he was so happy when democracy was restored! 'I'll come again,' he'd tell me every so often when we spoke on the phone, 'I'll come again, now everything will change, bad things never last long in Greece,' that's what he kept saying . . . You're his grandson, right?

[9] In 1967, a coup d'état established a military dictatorship in Greece, which was overthrown in 1974.

Do you look like him, sonny? Bless you, my boy, and give Erasmia and your sister a kiss from me, is your mother nearby? Can I speak to her?"

"This isn't a good time," I said, "everyone's busy," and I hung up the phone.

I went back to the stained couch. They said that with the blood a girl becomes a woman. Will you change now, Amalia? Will you be more reserved, more shy, more what? Will you leave me? Tell me, won't we run together in the park anymore, won't we chase squirrels, won't we fall over each other on the grass, panting for breath? Won't you kiss me on the neck? Won't you tell me:

"Hey, your squirrel got away!"

"No, here he is, standing and looking at us; it was yours that disappeared into the leaves."

"No, Jonathan, nothing will change."

And yet, something did change. Love became forbidden.

* * *

Chestnuts, oaks, ashes, poplars, willows, copses of firs, apple trees in bloom—do you know how many thousands of trees and wildflowers our park has? And lakes, and skating rinks, and bridle paths, and trails for horse-drawn carriages and bicycles, and merry-go-rounds—it was heaven on earth, Amalia, what fun we used to have there! Never mind how Grandpa would go on about that other park where he came from, the Royal Garden which they renamed the National Garden, how "it may not have so many trees and it certainly doesn't have any squirrels, but it's still a lovely garden."

"Its paths are like a maze, you can find cool and shady hideaways and lush vegetation, and then suddenly, as you're walking along, you might come across a peacock. We'll go there one day, all of us together, it'll be lovely," Grandpa would say. "Now everything is different back home," he'd say. We never went. On my own, without you, I'll be landing there in five hours and seventeen minutes. What will I find there? There are no squirrels in the Garden and when night falls the guards close the gate to the Sacred Rock of the Acropolis. I'll be arriving in the evening.

"One day we'll go together," Menelaos used to say.

"Why not now, Grandpa?" I asked him one

day. "You keep saying we'll go, so let's do it this summer."

"The later we go, the better it'll be," he replied.

And he was so thrilled when Seraphim's son decided to come and see us. So thrilled. But after he left, Grandpa would say, "One day we'll all go there together," less and less. You'd hear him say, "It'll be lovely there," less and less.

Grandpa's face lit up when he saw Sakis, his nephew. He was elated! The son of his cousin Seraphim. "He's a grown man, how quickly the years have gone by"—food and desserts were prepared, Erasmia got dressed up, our house became festive. It was the fall of 1995.

"Let's make sure he has a good time, as if Seraphim himself were here, let's take him to the Empire State Building, to the piers, to the Met and the MoMa and the Guggenheim," said Mama, "there's an interesting exhibition on there. If it's sunny, we can take the ferry to the piers, he can cross the Brooklyn Bridge on a bicycle, we can go to the Blue Note in the Village, we can go and see *Cats*, we can take him to the zoo, and the Ice Capades, and Chinatown for Peking duck, and for a walk through Astoria so he can see our old neighborhood."

Sakis chose to stay at the Plaza. It was his first time in New York.

"Nice apartment, uncle," Sakis said on the one and only time he came to our house, "and in a first class neighborhood too." He'd heard that Riverside Drive was a good part of town. "You've made a bundle, haven't you, uncle? Fortunately, your cousin Seraphim has his health and he's lived to see me do pretty well for myself, although he is a little weird and doesn't quite get me, he's a little stuck in the past, but he's okay, he makes me laugh despite his eighty years, you know what that can be like, of course, you folks are lucky, living here in the center of the universe!" Grandpa listened to him, looking lost. As if he were trying to understand things that were beyond him. "And life has changed for the better now, uncle, you won't recognize the old country. You can't imagine the construction going on, and if one day we get to hold the Olympic Games, and it's very possible that we will, uncle, then you'll see development and progress like you won't believe! We won't recognize our poor old Greece! Wouldn't it be a good idea for you to come and visit after all these years?"

I saw Grandpa hesitating and a worried look

passing over Grandma's eyes. Then Sakis turned to you and said:

"Play something on the piano, kiddo, and let me hear your voice, I've heard you have an amazing voice."

You were ready to do him the favor, but Mama sprang to her feet, "Our little Amalia is tired today, and she has a sore throat, better that she doesn't sing," she said. "Better not," you echoed and she—do you remember, Amalia?—walked to the door, said, "If you'll excuse me," and hurried out.

She came back late that night . . . I woke up . . . I heard her crying . . . What's going on with our mother, Amalia? What is it that's eating her up inside?

Sakis didn't waste his time on us. He had other plans. He didn't want to do anything we'd come up with.

"I'll wander around the stores on my own, I have the addresses right here," he said, and took out a crocodile-skin Filofax. "I'll go to Fifth Avenue, I have all the addresses I need." And proudly he showed us an endless list of names: Bergdorf Goodman, Carolina Herrera, Celine, Cerruti, Gucci, Intermix, Krizia, Saks, Ferragamo,

Takashimaya, and Valentino. "I'll spare you the hassle of coming along; it'll take me hours to pick out suits and presents."

He asked us if we knew of a place that makes custom-tailored shirts so he could have his monogram embroidered on them, and, oh yes, he also wanted to get the latest cell phone. Amalia, you looked at him with empty eyes, your eyes looked just like hers, the yellow in your eyes, with that hint of gold. For a moment your eyes and Mama's eyes seemed the same. You wanted to do as she had done. To say excuse me, and to disappear. But, Amalia, you were fourteen years old and sudden departures were not permitted. So you remained, as did I, in the living room with our guest. If your eyes could speak, they would have said a prayer for the wrongful death of a little crocodile and asked: *How did that little crocodile, that swam happily in lakes and swamps, end up becoming a cover for our guest's personal organizer? And how could you ever sing and play the piano in front of a little dead crocodile?*

Sakis was a sales representative. Ah, Seraphim, I don't know if that's what you dreamed your son would become. He even suggested he and Grandpa go into business together.

"We can get into security systems, uncle. In Greece now everyone wants to protect their windows with aluminum bars so they can sleep soundly at night, like in the old times," he said. "We should work together, uncle, we'll make a pile."

Grandpa looked at him, at a loss, and said nothing . . . And when Sakis got up to leave, saying, "Cousin Frosso and I will go out on the town one night," Grandpa seemed afraid for some reason to show his unease. So he kept it inside and said, "Yes, of course, nephew, that's a good idea." And it was then that I sensed that Grandpa's life was ebbing and that he wouldn't be with us for much longer.

At home one day we had an emergency. Grandpa woke up as if he were someone else. Grandma kept speaking to him but he remained mute.

"Menelaos, your coffee's ready. Would you like a muffin? A bagel?"

Menelaos didn't make a sound.

"Grandpa, talk to us. Do you want some bread?"

He sat there motionless, as if made of stone. Could he not hear us? Could he not understand us? We feared the worst. A stroke. We were prepared. Even us kids. At school we'd been trained in first aid. If it was a stroke, we had to think of the word. "Remember the first three letters, STR: S (smile), T (talk), R (raise)."

Smile: Tell him to smile.

Talk: Tell him to say a simple sentence, like "Today is a sunny day."

Raise: Tell him to raise his arms.

"Grandpa, smile. Say, 'Today is Thursday, my name is Menelaos.' Raise your arms."

Nothing. His face was like a death mask. Immobile, motionless. And just as Grandma, all flustered, began calling for an ambulance, Grandpa took her hand.

"Don't bother with a doctor, Erasmia. It's not necessary. Here, look at me, I'm smiling," he said and grimaced. "Today is Thursday, my name is Menelaos Argyriou. Here are my two arms and I'm raising them. My time has yet to come." He looked each one of us in the eye. In a tired voice, he added: "I'm sad, I'm not sick. Don't confuse sadness and sickness."

"Praise the Lord!" said Grandma with a sigh of relief and Anthoula made the sign of the cross.

"Everything's okay," said Mama and went out, while we left for school.

But Grandpa's time wasn't far off. It wasn't

with a stroke but with sadness that Menelaos said goodbye to life. He was sad that "over there" a man like Sakis was living and growing and prospering. Sakis and his crocodile Filofax.

* * *

"We are entering an area of turbulence. Please return to your seats and fasten your seat belts."

"Sir, the sign is on, please buckle up, we're entering turbulence."

"Thank you, I'm so sorry. I didn't notice it."

If you ever have a child, don't give it a dead person's name. Give your child a name without a past, Amalia.

"Me? Have a child? You're talking craziness again, Jonathan."

* * *

She was lying on the couch, it was in the afternoon and we'd just got back from school, she was dozing. She had already changed her name. She had begun to drink like a fiend. She kept stashing little bottles—so that they'd fit anywhere—of whiskey in the bathroom, in the throw pillows, in your room. One day, "What's this?" you asked, you didn't know. You found a little bottle in the belly of one of your dolls.

"It's nothing," said Grandma. She snatched the bottle from your hands. "It got there by mistake," she said.

Why did they lie to us? What was the truth they were hiding from us?

Mama got up from the couch, any sleepiness had disappeared from her face. She shoved Grandma angrily. "It didn't get there by mistake," she shouted. "I put it there, it's mine."

"What is it, Mama, what's inside?"

"Medicine."

"Why did you put it here? You ruined Marlena's dress, her belly button's sticking out, look," and you pointed at the hole in the belly of your huge doll and there was anger in your face, "you're bad," you yelled at her, "I don't love you."

"I'm bad, but you be good," she said, and shut herself in her room.

We could hear nothing, what were we waiting

for? Sobs? Sighs? It became quiet. That woman's tears never had a voice. Silence.

"I'll buy you another doll," said Grandma.

"I want that one," you declared, and from that moment on I only cared about one thing; ever since I can remember myself, I only wanted one thing: that you should never have anything broken, nothing with holes in it, nothing ruined. But our story was full of holes. And Grandma was too old to fill them, Anthoula too clumsy, and Grandpa . . . for some time now, Grandpa had been preparing for his big journey.

You were seven and I was nine. A story ran on inside us. Children can endure all kinds of stories. They're saving their strength for what is to come.

Who was our father? In the beginning, I called Menelaos "daddy," and no one said:

"Wrong, that's your grandpa, don't call him 'daddy' again."

Menelaos never got angry and never corrected me when I called him "daddy." It made him happy, and sad, and frightened, and I could see all these things in his eyes, Amalia, I'm telling you the truth, I was just a little kid and I could see that a person is never a single one, but lots of people together, and the things people have inside them are many and muddled up, and it's this "lots of people together" that makes us want one another. Whoever our father was, he never came.

"He lives far away, he lives elsewhere," they'd tell us.

"Elsewhere where, in which country?"

"He's always traveling, he has no country."

"Why isn't he with us?"

"Because he can't be in one place, he suffers too much."

"Why doesn't he come for the day?"

"He's afraid that he may not be able to leave afterwards, that he'll grow attached to you."

"And what if he does? And what if he stays? And what if we all stay together?"

"He'll be like a dead man."

"Show us a picture if him."

"There is no picture of him."

So then I'd say to myself: *Daddy is the man who stays inside Mama's body and never appears, but he's there, enchanted by a woman, circulating inside her like blood, and in exchange filling his belly with her warmth.*

Did we have the same father? Did she meet him secretly? On certain rare occasions perhaps, when he interrupted his absence and would come to meet her, always far from the house, so that he wouldn't see me, so that he wouldn't lay eyes on his son and grow attached to him and then not be able to leave, and once, during a secret, amorous encounter, one that was a little more desperate, a little more unbearable than the others, when they made love like it was the last time, then it was your turn to be born, Amalia, and we were both the children of a great, impossible love, that's what I'd tell myself. And this thought made me feel better.

"*You were always in love with dreams, Jonathan.*"

We lived with an invisible father.

"*In order to love a human being, Jonathan, they have to be invisible. Otherwise, as soon as they appear, love disappears.*"

Then you were no longer a baby . . . Whenever you'd see a man, you'd say "daddy, you daddy" and then "father" and you'd learned to say "babá" in Greek, "hush, Amalia," "stop it, Amalia, stop it," we don't know this gentleman, he's the delivery boy, the porter, Grandpa's employee, the bus driver, a homeless man on the street, a carriage driver in Central Park, a mounted policeman, a . . . Nobody is your daddy, Amalia, and only she knows who he is.

And then one morning, on Thanksgiving Day, the day when families come together, "You're grown children now, it's time to learn the truth," she said.

"No, we're not grown children yet, we need more time, let us not be grown children for a little while longer, I'm eleven and my sister's barely nine."

But she refused to be swayed, not even when I told her:

"The truth is for the very old, Mama, and maybe not even for them."

"Your father died of a heart attack," she announced. "He was fifty-four years old, his name was John Merida."

During the following days, she kept changing the name and the story:

"Your father was a war hero, his name was John Carrey."

"Your father was a businessman, his name was Peter Allison; he died in a plane crash."

You suddenly stopped calling every man you met "father." Orphan children feed on stories. We grew up on them. We went over them in our heads, bringing them to life. Words, even when they were marked by pain, stole our pain away.

* * *

Sixty years earlier, the other Frosso had a hard time making up stories, she didn't want to, she was a mere girl of twenty-two, she didn't want the big dream, she wanted the little one, her own tiny little dream, the garden, the rosebushes, the cyclamens were what she wanted, they sprang out of the ground with the first rain and their fragrance drove her wild, she wanted to be driven wild by the smells of the earth, she wanted the sea she remembered, the sea that bathed her eyes from afar and gave moisture to her body . . . The poverty she knew—she yearned for all those things she knew. But Menelaos would say, "Frosso, we'll die if we stay here," and he took her away, he carried her off, as soon as they were married, together with her bundle of clothes and belongings, the first time she saw the sea up close was at Piraeus, she was frightened by the crowds, the music, the municipal band was playing, was it a celebration or a memorial service for a dead official? The ship was like a moored beast, the biggest thing she'd ever seen in her life. It was immense. It would take her into its belly, for twenty-one days it would take her on a journey "far away." She had her heart in her mouth, "I don't want to go," she whispered, but he was having none of it, with the tickets in his hand he dragged her along, "Come on, my little Frosso, we're late," she screeched, "I won't go, I want my mama, I won't go," "Are you stark raving mad, woman? Your mother's been dead for years," "I want her, I'm not getting on." Menelaos grew angry, "You're getting on and you're going to like it." Then he thought he'd try and cajole her, "Come on, baby girl, why don't you sing a song to cure what ails you with that voice of an angel that you have, come on, my sweet, sing a song and forget your sorrows, sing, my angel," oh, Amalia, there are no such songs . . . such songs were never written on this earth . . . only the band could be heard, playing a jaunty march . . . people were embracing, Greek and American flags were waving . . . it was a spring day and the sky was clear. Soon, the ship's horn gave the signal, the ship slipped her moorings, and the voyage to the dream began. It was nine o'clock in the morning. Shortly after, the blood spoke. What cyclamen and what sea and what fragrance of honeysuckle and lemon? They found themselves crammed into a dark hold, and it smelled of sweat, and coal, and something scorched; it smelled of an animal's wounded flesh.

"I can't breathe, Menelaos, I can't breathe, my mama's telling me something, can you hear, my ears are stuffed up, she's telling me something, she's giving me something, what is it, it's a handkerchief, a handkerchief with flowers, take it for me, my hands, I can't feel my hands, take the handkerchief, I tell you, my ears are cold, I'm freezing, I'm going up on deck, I'm going to the bridge, I can't take it in here." She's three levels below deck and she goes up the stairs. Eyes look at her hatefully and others just sadly, gazes of all kinds follow her, yet her own eyes are nowhere, but lo, here's her mama now, following her to the bridge, giving her the hankie, she doesn't need Menelaos, she needs her mama.

"Be careful you don't catch cold, girl."

"Don't you worry, Mama."

"Frosso, my little one, it's cold there, they tell me, it's no laughing matter, everything is laughless there."

"Yes, Mama."

"There are no dovecotes there or churches carved into the rocks, but Menelaos loves you."

"Yes, Mama."

"You must love him too."

"Yes, Mama."

"Don't cause him more worries, he's got enough on his mind. And take care of your voice. Keep singing, my little Frosso, you have a voice from God, remember, 'a golden loom and an ivory comb / and the body of an angel,' you were five years old and everybody adored your voice."

And then her mama went back to her own affairs and little Frosso saw the eyes of strangers, the lice, the filth, the deck covered in vomit, the bodies crammed together like orphan animals, she saw the chimney spewing out smoke, and then she could see nothing else, only the blackness of the smoke that enveloped her . . . and she flung herself from the bridge with the handkerchief tied tightly around her hair. It was the seventh day of the voyage, in ten days Menelaos would arrive in a foreign land, alone, with a bundle that was much lighter. He kept a dress of hers as a souvenir, the rest he gave away, and then he took the ship back to Greece.

A story ran on inside us. Children can endure all kinds of stories. They're saving their strength for what is to come.

* * *

Sakis left. With a phone call and a "we didn't manage it, maybe next time, you live in a wonderful city, it's a shame Frosso and I didn't get together, we will next time, either here or there." He left and went back over there and there was no next time.

Grandpa didn't live much longer after Sakis left. He died in February 1996.

"I want to talk to you, but make sure you're alone, without your sister, you're a man now, you'll understand." It was a Saturday, the fourth day without Menelaos. "It's something I've been wanting to tell you for a long time."

Not a man, Grandma, no, let me not be a man for a little longer, let me not understand, I'm only sixteen years old, Grandma, I haven't been with a woman yet and at school I struggle with the forbidden words and now the house smells different, it smells of vodka not whiskey, because vodka has no smell and it won't betray you.

But I smelled it, in the bathroom, and in her bedroom, and in the kitchen, and in the elevator, I smelled it and I knew that our mother was drinking and running away again. And Grandma Erasmia insisted on talking to me and she locked the kitchen door in case you or Mama walked in and overheard us, "Only you," she said, and I, who wished to have no secrets from you, Amalia, was forced to say:

"All right, I'll keep it a secret."

"Your sister is young, I don't want her to know."

"I promise," I said, "I promise I'll keep it to myself," even though I knew that keeping it to myself smelled of loneliness and death, and that nothing has yet to exist in this world, Amalia, that I would want to keep to myself.

"We'd better go outside. Let's take a walk."

She unlocked the door. She took me by the hand. We went to the park. Next to the lake, we sat on a bench. A metal plaque stuck to its back said: "In memory of Tom Singer, beloved husband and father." At our feet was the lake and its ducks, squirrels were scampering across the grass. It was a sunny day, horse-drawn carriages, joggers, cyclists went by, a saxophone was playing, it was delightful.

"I had your mother when I was almost forty," she began, as she sat next to me, speaking in a calm and determined tone. "I'd been trying for over ten years, absolutely nothing, 'It's not God's will,' I'd tell myself. 'And Frosso up there probably doesn't want it.' My daughter was to take her name. The child I would have would be a girl, no question. No doubt in my mind about that. And she would take her name. In ten years, I'd dreamed of my sister three times.

"'Don't do this to me,' she'd said, 'don't bring me back to life. I'm fine here.'

"But once again I didn't listen to her, Jonathan. Once again, I only thought of myself. Like I had back then, like I have always. With the daughter I'd have, I'd bring her back to life, do you get what I'm saying, Jonathan, tell me, do you get what I'm saying? Not only would she have her name, but she'd also have her beauty and her grace, her eyes, her hair. Oh, Jonathan, you can't imagine Frosso's face, yes, she looked exactly like your mother, exactly the same. I'm going to Hell, Jonathan, and if there is no Hell, it'll be made to exist just for me. I disobeyed my sister a second time, when she left with Menelaos and it was as if my homeland and my home had burned down a second time, because how would my life be without her, without my little Frosso, and yet at the same time jealousy was gnawing at me, here she was, going off to a new land, with a husband, a handsome strong husband, she was off to a new continent, her eyes would see such marvels, she'd be leaving behind this war that was about to break out and everything that would come in its wake, she wouldn't know the hunger, the savagery, the fear, the bombs exploding next to us, the conquering army in our neighborhood and in our home, she wouldn't live through the Occupation, and—the time has come for me to reveal it to you, Jonathan, my beloved grandson—as soon as little Frosso left, it was as if this sharp pain made me see everything that would happen to our country, I don't know how or why, I saw before me death approaching, I'm not afraid of my words, Jonathan, no one about to die is afraid of revelations, and mark my words, I won't be around for much longer, so anyway, on that first night, when I was left alone in the empty house, I got on my knees to say my prayers, as we always did with little Frosso, 'God of our homeland, rest the souls of all those who were not fortunate enough to come here with us, Mama and Papa and all those who were lost in the scorched land.' But my lips, as if of their own accord, whispered something else that night: 'God of our homeland, make

something happen, please, make something—
anything—happen, some inconceivable and unre-
stricted and unlimited something is what I'm asking for. Make something happen so that I leave
here and go and live in America, just get me out
of here.' And God answered my prayer, Jonathan,
and that's why I'm going to Hell, unless it was the
Devil who heard me, which makes my god the
Devil, and what can I say . . . What can I say . . .
What more can I say . . . The Devil-God
answered my prayer, my little Frosso was out of
my life, and as if that wasn't enough, I won't just
let her be, even when she tells me she's fine, I
want to bring her back, as if then my sins would
be blotted out and forgotten, through a young
girl, my daughter, whom I will name after her.
And that's what I did, Jonathan, and twelve years
later the new Frosso was born, my daughter. Your
mama, Jonathan, your beautiful, accursed mama,
your dead mama, Jonathan. One day, when she
had become a young girl, she put on a miniskirt
that barely covered her underwear, the whole
house shone with youth and innocence, she put
on her first pair of tights, black silk, that she'd
bought from the Saks boutique, and a blouse
which was open at the chest, it was March and

spring was awakening in the Big Apple, your mother was thirteen years old and her chest had begun to awaken and not fit into her old clothes, and I saw Menelaos, your grandpa, in the dining room, I saw the gleam in his eye as he stood before his daughter so resplendent, 'Frosso,' he said, and as God, as the Devil's my witness, as either of the two is my witness, or both of them in one, I caught in the air that the name 'Frosso' didn't refer to his daughter, but to his dead first wife, my sister, and that his voice was filled with lust and sexual yearning, Jonathan, a father for his daughter, Jonathan, and we'll all burn together, Jonathan, it was the same voice that I had heard twenty-six years earlier on Ergasias Street in New Ionia, telling my sister: 'Frosso, I'm going to make you my wife.' He felt it too and it upset him no end, and from then on he began to work late more and more and to stay at home less and less. He was growing old fast, I knew I wouldn't have him for much longer. And your mother, who knew nothing, it was as if she knew everything. When we went to Athens, she didn't even want to hear about coming with us. 'I'll stay here.' She was the same age Amalia is now. When we came back, it was as if years had gone by, even though we'd only been away barely a month. You had to be told all these things."

"Let's go home, Grandma, the sun's gone down, let's go home."

"*My sweet Jonathan!*"

It was you I was thinking of, Amalia, the whole time Grandma was talking, I kept thinking how you must never find out.

"*How naïve can you be, Jonathan? Did it never occur to you that there were no secrets? We all knew. We all pretended not to know what we knew.*"

But I . . . Amalia, I . . . I . . .

"*You?*"

I love you, Amalia.

"*You're attracted to death, why don't you relax in your seat, you still have a few more hours of traveling ahead of you, look at how calmly your fellow passengers are enjoying their flight, there, there now, just shut out my memory.*"

Everything was changing, Amalia. Grandpa was no longer with us. We were growing up, we graduated high school, you were studying music at college and I was trying to find myself, making plans I never went through with. At home, Bellino had given his place to Demosthenes, whom you had found as a newborn one day near the river. Unlike Bellino, he would sit at your feet for hours, purring. The white couch was worn; dust and damp covered the old stains. The smell of alcohol had faded. Mother hadn't stopped drinking, she'd just switched from whiskey to vodka.

One day, Grandma moved out. *She* did it: Lale Andersen. Without asking us, without thinking it over, she just decided that Grandma wouldn't be living with us anymore. Her new address was the Serenity nursing home in Upper Manhattan.

"They'll take better care of her there," she told us.

Anthoula also left. We didn't need her anymore, she said, and sent her off to some relatives of hers in Astoria. She didn't care what we thought. One evening, just like that, without warning, when we came home, Grandma was gone.

"Starting today, your grandma doesn't live here anymore," she announced.

"What do you mean?" I asked.

You went straight to the piano and began to play.

"*I couldn't bear to listen, Jonathan, I just couldn't bear it.*"

"Why did you do it, Mama?"

"She's protected there. Here everything's . . . everything's . . . open, open windows, drafts, noises. She'll have peace and quiet there."

You started playing louder, Amalia, banging on the keys ferociously. Demosthenes cowered in a corner.

"I couldn't bear to listen, Jonathan. I just couldn't bear it."

I felt the anger welling up inside me.

"Whatever you feel like doing," I threw in her face, "whatever harebrained idea you get into your head, who are you to decide about our lives, who the hell are you?"

And it all came pouring out of me at once. I asked her about our father. For the first time.

"Who is he? Forget the lies you've been feeding us all these years and just tell us."

"What does it matter?"

"How dare you? Who are you to decide what matters?"

She began mumbling something.

"He's a stranger, I didn't want it to go any further, an unknown father leaves no traces. I didn't want any traces."

"Was he indigent? Homeless? At the Blue

Mountain there was a man who called me his son, was it him?"

"I don't know."

"Was it the same stranger with Amalia?"

"Yes."

"Is she my full sister? Same mother, same father?"

"Yes."

"Why don't you just die?"

That was when you stopped playing, Amalia, your fingers, which had been running wildly over the keys, stopped in midair. "I'm leaving," you said, but you didn't, you stayed there, looking down at the piano keys as if you had kept on playing.

"Why don't you just die?"

She looked at me without moving. Like a statue. As if gazing at me from afar. She bowed her head, touched her chin, and I remembered the funerary stele at the museum.

"Why don't you just die?"

She began speaking gibberish. I couldn't understand what she was saying.

"*No, Jonathan, it's not true, don't play hide and seek with your memory. Mama answered you, she didn't speak gibberish at all, she said:*

"*'I can't die because dead people don't die, I can't*

die because I'm already dead, from the moment I took the place of a dead woman. My family saw to my death before I was even born.'

"*That was what our mother said, Jonathan. And it was then that I stopped playing, I stood up and left the room, remember?*"

It's been a long time, Amalia.

"*Fourteen years, Jonathan. January 2013. You're traveling to our land of origin.*"

Amalia, you shouldn't have . . .

"*There's no such thing as should or shouldn't have, Jonathan. Who are we to say? Who are we to change it? The destiny of the world is more important than our own.*"

Once or twice a week I would visit Grandma. She was growing old with a quiet dignity. Her health was good and her mind was in fine form for her age. At first, you'd come along too, but then you stopped visiting. I would go alone.

"*Grandma wanted you there alone, Jonathan, my presence prevented her from speaking.*"

Eight years went by. Menelaos's diner was sold to an Italian. Its name was changed from "Ellinis" to "Bella Napoli." Once a month you played piano there and sang. Your friends would come along, Michael, too. Music won you over. You kept practicing and playing the piano. And I would sit and read for hours on end and look for a job to justify my existence. We were too old to go roller skating or ice skating, too old to feed the squirrels in the park and play hide and seek with them, too old to ask: "Mama, where do you drift off to, why won't you speak to us?" The colorful crowd was always there, in the streets, on the avenues, despite the unbearable winter cold and the stifling summer heat, the crowd was unfailingly there. Noisy and detached from our story, the crowd flooded our city, which could never embrace us in its silence. We were growing up with this unchanged crowd. It was in its company that we ushered in the new millennium. At Times Square, the universe was ablaze, thousands of fireworks embroidering the sky, "Happy New Millennium," "Happy 2000." We put on paper hats, we blew on party horns and waved American flags, we burrowed into the pandemonium. The sky was turning red. I saw you with Michael, he had his arm around you.

"He was just a friend, Jonathan, nothing more, you glared at him like he was a thief."

No stranger could ever make you happy, Amalia.

"You needn't have worried. Happiness and I never got along that well, Jonathan."

My head grew heavy. I couldn't take any more celebrations. I went home hoping no one was there. But she was there. Alone. Drinking. She offered me a glass of champagne.

"Happy New Year, son!" she said.

"Happy New Year, Miss Andersen!" I downed the drink with one gulp and went to bed.

It was January 1st, 2000. I went to visit Grandma.

In a clean room, a TV set, a table, an armchair, soon she'd turn eighty-five, there was no room or need for anything more. Every two hours a nurse made a cursory check—blood pressure cuff, oxygen tank, serum IV at the ready, urine sample cups. The dining room was on the lower floor, there was a young volunteer who'd wheel her down there, "She's absolutely fine," the head nurse assured me. In a corner on the windowsill, among the skyscrapers, a little plastic plant pot with a flower that looked like a cyclamen stood out like a sore thumb, no doubt a gift from Anthoula, no one else came to see her. "She's almost completely silent all day long," the volunteer said, and when I asked him, "And how about at night?" he didn't reply. I stroked her hair like you would have. She was sitting in the armchair, I couldn't tell if she was sleeping. I adjusted a lock of her white hair which fell limply to the side. She half opened her eyes and gave a faint smile.

"Amalia, is that you?" she said.

"It's not Amalia, it's Jonathan, Grandma."

"Frosso?"

"It's Jonathan, Grandma."

I didn't stay. Next day, the exact same thing. As soon as she saw me, she sat up in bed, and when I touched her hair, with lifeless eyes and an almost nonexistent voice, she said:

"Amalia, is that you?"

"Yes, Grandma, it's Amalia, didn't you recognize me?"

With something that looked like a smile on her lips, she whispered:

"But of course I recognize you, what a thing to ask, come and sit next to me, *canım*."[10]

"I put on your eyes and I caressed her, Amalia."

"But, Jonathan, you told the truth."

The turbulence persists, growing heavier. The

[10] *My soul.*

flight attendant takes the glass of red wine that has just spilled over the white napkin that was spread on my lap. When Grandpa ate, he would always tie a white napkin around his neck. Do you remember, Amalia? Grandma also had a white napkin tied around her neck, the volunteer had just finished feeding her.

"She didn't make a mess at all," he said to me. "We did really well."

A few days went by and I went back to see her. It was as if there was someone else in her place. The young volunteer was waiting for me.

"She's restless," he said, "very restless." And then added: "She's been waiting for you."

"Whom?" I asked anxiously. "Whom has she been waiting for?"

"You, of course. Aren't you her grandson?"

"Yes, I am," and I asked him to step outside for a bit.

Grandma Erasmia lay there with her eyes wide open, without looking at me, and she opened her mouth and words, meanings, her broken-down regained train of thought began to pour out like the sea.

"I don't like skyscrapers, they make our souls dizzy, I never got used to them, did you know that?"

"Yes, Grandma."

"I'd look at the Empire State Building and the Twin Towers and all these tall buildings and I'd close my eyes, and then I'd see stone houses and dovecotes and carved churches."

"Calm down, Grandma, stop thinking now, stop remembering."

"How easy it is to leave, easier than one might imagine . . . I'm ready now, I'm ready, *şimdi bu akşam.*"[11]

"What are you talking about, Grandma? You're going to be fine, we'll go back home, Mama's waiting for you, and so is Amalia, they couldn't come today, Amalia wasn't feeling well, they're getting the house all spruced up, they're expecting you. From the moment you left, Demosthenes has lost his appetite and won't come out from under the bed, can you believe it? Everyone can't wait for you to come home!"

"Yes, yes, *evet,*[12] I know, *biliyorum kalbim,*[13] Menelaos, Frosso and Little Frosso, Amalia, Seraphim and Sakis. But they're also waiting for

---

[11] *Now, tonight.*
[12] *Yes.*
[13] *I know, my heart.*

me: Isidoros, Avraam, Katina, Anastasia, Aglaia, Nikitas, Cemal, Hassan, Spyros. Hills covered in orange groves, fairy caves, it smells of lavender and lemon, it'll be so bright, white and red together. The sun setting in the sky, not a scorching fire." She was gasping for breath. "Tall buildings and skyscrapers make me dizzy, you know they do, tell me that yes, you know."

"Yes, Grandma, I know."

"Fatma, Şehrazat, Bulent, Özgur, Onur, Tarik, Nazlı, they all want to come and see me, and Mehmet with his oud from Talas."

"No, Grandma, no, catch your breath," but there was no taming her tongue as she tried to get all the names in, "no," I pressed my hand to her lips, "no," I wet her lips with some water, "no . . . no . . . " A torrent of names came gushing out, it would have swallowed us both up if I had let it, we would have drowned, Amalia.

A crazy child thought its mother was many mothers in one. It screamed that she had two heads. The mean one would try to eat the child, while the other was tender and compassionate. The child sang while it was being slaughtered, singing to the blood it was losing.

She suddenly stopped, exhausted . . . *Oh my*

God . . . it'll happen now, I said to myself, and I've never been with someone at the end, I don't know how strong I am, how much I can take, how fearful I might be . . . I know nothing about myself, Amalia . . . I am here . . . but I'd like to run far away, somewhere else, to another country . . . to leave her here alone to settle her accounts with God . . .

She held onto me . . . She grabbed my arm tightly by the wrist—where did she find so much strength in that skinny body?

"Don't go," she said, forcefully. "No one else will want to help me. Stay. Sit by me. I'm scared. Don't listen to what I was saying earlier, when I pretended to be brave. There's nobody more scared on this earth than me. D'you hear me?"

"But why?"

"Because once I wished someone dead, a loved one, my most loved. I wished for it."

"Grandma, we've all wished that, there isn't a person alive who hasn't wished someone they loved dead."

"But with me it's different," she said.

"Why?"

"Because she actually died, she drowned . . . I took her place. What I dreamed came true. My daughter (love her as much as you can!), my daughter is protecting me. Let her drink, my boy, she drowns in booze and it calms her soul, my daughter's hiding from me so that I don't see her and have horrible images awaken inside me, she doesn't come to see me so as not to make me remember, it's out of kindness that she hides from me, she was only a little girl and I would hug her and she'd avoid me, it was out of kindness that she didn't want me to love her, to keep me from being sad, to make me see her as a stranger and not as my daughter and my sister both, as living and dead both, my daughter became hardhearted for my sake, it was I, it was I, well, not I, but our story, Jonathan . . . Who are we to set out to change our history? My daughter hard-hearted? Don't you ever say that again about your mother, hardness often hides kindness, we're only a toy in the hands of history, that's what we are, a toy, an insignificant little toy, *başka dünya yok*,[14] my daughter's just like her, my daughter's punishing me, have they forgiven me? Who can tell me? I didn't want to stay in Greece, I wanted to get out of there, after my

[14] There is no other world.

sister left with Menelaos, how was I supposed to stay on in Podarades? How could I suffer a second uprooting? Soon after, the war would break out, in a war people are divided. Friends, neighbors, relatives. Nikitas would be with the good guys, Costas would be with the bad guys, they'd change their names, their clothes, their smell, their voices, the good guys would become bad guys, the bad guys would deceive us using foreign kindnesses, there'd be that smell of burning again, everything would go back to the fire, again I'd see red across the sky and I wouldn't be able to tell if it was a beautiful sunset or a fire and roofs of houses being torched, I wanted to leave, to leave. What's true, what's a lie, what's a beautiful sunset and what's a fire that burns and destroys? I'm afraid, Jonathan. The story will never stop repeating itself. That's how people are made; it's human nature not to be able to prevent repetition. That's what 'human being' means: that which cannot prevent repetition. Even more than death, Jonathan, what I fear is repetition. So does your mother. She's learned to dread repetition too. Terror, I'm to blame, I'm to blame, fear, I'm to blame, I'm to blame, fear, I'm to blame, I'm to blame, fear, fear, fear . . . "

"I'm not surprised, Jonathan, given everything you've told me."

I stayed with her till the end. Grandma became lost in her delirium, mumbling words from a first language which she believed had been forgotten. *Annem seni çok özledim, başka dünya yok, kalbim sizin için yandı.*[15]

Death, Amalia, isn't that death? To lose yourself in your delirium?

"A good death, Jonathan."

Inside us, Grandma continues . . .

" *. . . to exist."*

I can see her, Amalia, I can see Little Frosso on her honeymoon, she's onboard the ocean liner "New Greece," carrying immigrants across the Atlantic, a newlywed, with Menelaos and her bundle with her belongings, she's said goodbye to her sister, six days later on the ship I run into her . . .

"It's no use, Jonathan, quiet down, you can't live the death of another."

I can't stop, Amalia. My memory has gone off the rails. I can see the scene unfolding before my eyes: "New Greece," 3rd class deck, June 1940.

---

[15] Mama, I've missed you so much, there is no other world, my heart pines for you.

"Menelaos, I'll just leave you for a moment, to get a drink of water, I'm thirsty, the way they have us cooped up in here, we're like prisoners in this stuffy hold, we're not travelers, this is anything but a honeymoon, I never imagined our voyage would be like this, Menelaos, I didn't . . . I'm only a little girl, Menelaos, I'm not made for goodbyes, only that one time, with the rowboat, but I had Erasmia by my side, now I don't have her, I don't want this new land, Menelaos, I want New Ionia and my sister and the flowers in little earthenware pots, I watered them every morning, I don't want to go, Menelaos, look at how the sailors and the stewards are eyeing me, and our fellow travelers with their damaged eyes, the lice in their hair, I used to wash my hair every day, Menelaos, my hair smelled of jasmine and lavender just like my sister's, by the time we arrive there the lice will have ravaged my hair, it smells like vomit on deck, everyone's throwing up, and they look at me suspiciously, 'Who the hell are you, missy?' 'I'm Frosso, Menelaos's wife, we're going to America,' 'You can kid yourself all you want, missy, you're not going to America, you're going to Hell!' burning coal, I remember the fires, can you remember when you're five years old,

Menelaos? I say yes, you can remember, smells outlast time, when everything has gone, all that's left are smells, there's two in particular, the smell of something burned by fire and the smell of the saltiness of the sea, it is with these two smells that I will now take my leave, to become one with them, goodbye, Menelaos, look after Erasmia for me, this is as much as I could do, *göstereyim sana, maşallah . . .* "[16]

The flight attendant asks me if I have a foreign passport and she gives me a form to fill out for Customs.

Where will I be landing soon, Amalia? There used to be an island, in the South Pacific, in the Coral Sea, between Australia and the French territory of New Caledonia. On nautical charts it was called Sample Island. During a reconnaissance expedition, the cartographers never found it. Returning from their sea voyage, which lasted twenty-five days, they said, "That's odd, this island is nowhere to be found." Where will I be landing soon, Amalia? Does our country exist?

[16] *I'll show you, as God is my witness . . .*

The country I never visited and which only now have you allowed me to travel to? The country where Menelaos and Anthoula were born, the country that welcomed Erasmia and the other Frosso, the country our mother never knew—does it exist?

The paper Frosso gives me a faint smile. She's twenty-three years old. I hold her in my hands with tender care. Seventy years separate me from the time this photograph was taken, just before she jumped over the side into the frozen waters of the Atlantic. "God seals the hand of every man, that all men may know His work." The pilot tells us where we're flying over, it's night outside. With a magical depth gauge used to measure unexplored oceans, I dream of a voyage to the ocean floor. I'm equipped with scuba gear and a high resolution underwater camera. I swim, I sink, and at some point, inside a marine cave, I locate her body, nude, dressed in corals, seaweed, plankton, the skeletons of dead fish wrapped around her arms and legs, conches and seashells, a frozen liquid preventing decomposition, Frosso of 1940 is swimming on the bottom of the sea. I immortalize her with my camera. I know you won't believe me. I need proof. I develop the photograph.

"Calm yourself, my dear Jonathan. Proof is only for daydreamers."

Three hours and a bit to go. I'm the only passenger who hasn't closed his eyes, not even for a moment, except in order to see a forbidden film. PG-rated. In the place where the island was supposed to be, cartographers found a huge depth of one thousand four hundred meters. Had the island sunk in there? Or did it never exist?

Amalia, I'm feeling queasy . . . I never got used to the skyscrapers encircling us, I get vertigo when I look up at them from a window. An opening onto the void. I try to ignore the empty seat next to me.

"When will you stop pitying the Argyriou family, Jonathan?"

Don't talk as if you have a different name, you're an Argyriou too.

"But pity no longer touches me."

Amalia, my heart, don't stop talking to me.

"Someone once wrote that all happy families are happy in the same way and unhappy families are unhappy each in their own way."

I don't care what writers say, I want you, I mind being the same, not being unique, I love you. Don't stop talking to me.

"It's all in your head, Jonathan, you don't really love me, you love being unhappy."

You don't know what you're talking about.

"You love all that binds us to our history, you love all the things we never had."

Unhappiness doesn't concern me, I don't care about happiness. I could jump into the void, Amalia, right now. I could break the glass pane and hurl myself into the void with all my strength.

"You'll never do that, don't kid yourself. Make do with dreams. At least they're not bloody."

While I'm falling into the void and just before the darkness envelops me, in a flash of lucidity I'll see the same dream as that woman. As she was falling onto the train tracks, she dreamt of the caress of a childhood sea.

"Now you're pretending to be Anna Karenina, stop playing roles, Jonathan."

I love you.

"You love the roles you play. The role of the lovelorn exiled Greek brother, the son of an unknown father and an alcoholic mother, suits you perfectly."

Be quiet.

"You."

Me?

"*Yes, you.*"

I am you.

"*You'll be arriving soon, stop your daydreaming and turn your mind to something practical. Which hotel are you staying at? Where will you go as soon as day breaks? Till what time and along which streets will you wander tonight? Will you go to New Ionia, will you look for Grandpa's house, will you see if there's a hole in the ground or a multistory building, perhaps a shopping mall, and Sakis will be there, the owner, the doorman, perhaps even the security guard, and then you'll end up at the harbor? Will you see ghost ships unloading their passengers with their flags at half-mast, and other magnificent ships for happy tourists, their flags waving proudly? Will you leave the climb up to the Sacred Rock of the Acropolis for last? Will you have put on a clean shirt? How will you arrange the unknown images inside you, Jonathan? A country we know is one thing, but a country we imagine is quite another. You don't just get to know a country from what it has plenty of, from its monuments and its past, but also from what it is now missing. How foreign are you to this land? Try to go to the home for abandoned children. They need shoes. Choose the kids to whom you'll give what they're missing. Here are their names, and each one's age and shoe size:*

1. Petros, twenty months old, size 21
2. Vivi, three and a half years old, size 25
3. Haris, two years old, size 23
4. Nikos, twelve months old, size 20
5. Raphael, one and a half years old, size 19
6. Panayotis, one and a half years old, size 20
7. Elli, two years old, size 22
8. Nikos, twelve months old, size 18
9. Myrto, two years old, size 21
10. Anastasia, two years old, size 22
11. Yorgos, eight and a half years old, size 36
12. Siphis, six years old, size 30
13. Revecca, two years old, size 23
14. Yannis, ten months old
15. Andrianna, eleven months old
16. Stella-Rosa, seven months old
17. Elias, eleven months old
18. Nadia, nine months old
19. Marinos, nine months old
20. male, four months old
21. male, four months old
22. female, five months old
23. male, seven months old

*

Tell me, Jonathan, how will you decide, how will you choose which ones to leave barefoot and which ones to give shoes to? From the moment we were born, we struggled to get an answer, there's no compass, Jonathan, I suggest you pick five pairs of shoes at random, and make sure you don't meet the children themselves. They feel awkward when faced with their benefactors. Sometimes they become surly and refuse all donations, and other times they plead for a brief smile. Leave your gift and go. Don't watch it being received. You don't need to see young children coming to blows for a pair of shoes. You're traveling to a foreign country, Jonathan, get ready. You don't need to meet the traffickers of children's souls, those who sell their organs, their eyes, their hands, their hearts."

I can dream, Amalia, of the light. Light. Happy, well-fed and warmly-dressed children enjoying sandy beaches for a summer and spring that never end. Carefree, fearless children, and the future is a window open to the horizon. The hawkers of souls are nowhere to be seen. In the streets, people's breaths smell of jasmine and kindness.

"*Dreams have some nerve . . . Sweet dreams, Jonathan.*"

Travel advisories tell those traveling to Greece to be careful. Homeless folk and underfed children, people losing their jobs every day and others who decide to end it all, parents who hand their children over to institutions because they can't raise them. Graffiti on the walls: "I'm in torment," "I don't want to live." Is this our country, Amalia?

"'Don't go, it's absurd," I kept telling myself, pigeons feeding hungry pedestrians, people with empty eyes walking along, mumbling, do you really want to experience that? Demonstrators, tear gas and chemicals blinding you. Am I a madman? I'm a kid who never knew his father. Containers for babies used in the past are making a comeback. In special boxes fitted into the outside of hospital walls, mothers can leave their unwanted babies. Infants are abandoned on apartment block steps, in church courtyards, in public maternity hospitals.

"You always exaggerate, Jonathan, whether you're hopeful or pessimistic."

I love you, Amalia. Exaggeration is what love dresses in. Otherwise love withers like a foundling.

At night, when sleep takes us all into his arms, Amalia, we become homeless. All of us. A strange

fraternity, vast and endless, ties us to each other.
I close my eyes for a moment, I pull down the
shade. Amalia, you make me love whatever I
come across in this country. Our country, Amalia.
We'll disembark together. Together we'll wander
through its wounded streets. You bring a lullaby
to my lips . . . You make me transform myself,
and I have nothing but these disguises of mine,
you lend me women's and children's and infants'
clothing, my body is never left bare. I dress up as
a mother. You dress me, Amalia. Nakedness disappears. I see them lying down on the sidewalk,
Ermou Street, Omonia Square, Exarchia,
Theatrou Street, Gazi, along all the streets I studied on the map, and it's as if I have already walked
these streets countless times in my imagination, I
see them wrapped in blankets, in cardboard
boxes they call home, a heavy winter is on the
way, with snow and hail. Paper houses just soak
up the rain.

I bend down over their heads and whisper in an
unusual, almost unknown tongue:

My sweet boy, why aren't you sleeping?
Don't be afraid, your mama's here
I'll sing my lullaby for you

And all your fears will be gone
Sleep well, my son
I love you and I sing for you
This lullaby.[17]

I borrow your voice, Amalia. The voice of our mama, and Erasmia, and the other Frosso, all the women's voices come together in my voice.

But the truth is that I'm afraid of the freezing winter there. However much I borrow the magic of your voice, fear wins me over. I'll be on my own. How will I get along?

"*The land has surprises in store for us, Jonathan. Surprise is the antidote to fear. A crazy child thought its mother was many mothers in one. It screamed that she had two heads. The mean one would try to eat the child, while the other was tender and compassionate. The child sang while it was being slaughtered, singing to the blood it was losing. And the blood turned into song and light. Light made of amber.*

---

[17] This lullaby, in an almost unknown language spoken in the Republic of Udmurtia, in central Russia, is sung in the documentary film *Lullaby* by Victor Kossakovsky on Europe's homeless, which was made as part of the "Why Poverty" initiative.

Transformation is the magical medicine for our country."

Are you telling the truth?

"*The land has surprises in store for us, Jonathan. It's a good land. Do you remember Grandma's Halcyon Days? When winter went on for too long, she'd tell us that the weather there is different. In the heart of winter, in the cold weather and the rough seas, for a few days there's something like a short summer. Darkness hides itself, the wind subsides, the chill moves away, the sun warms the country, winter disappears into winter. The whole land looks after a bird.*"

It's a bird called Halcyon and it must hatch its eggs in the winter. Its eggs will hatch in nests in the rocks. It's wintertime, but there's a god who lets the sun shine brightly to keep the mother warm until her babies are born.

"*Yes, Jonathan, you're traveling there now. Winter might pause.*"

"We've started our descent into Athens. Please return to your seats."

I can dream, Amalia.

"*Now is the moment, Jonathan.*"

Takeoff and landing are the most dangerous parts of a flight. The pious woman in front lets out a little screech.

"We're almost there," she says with relief.

"Yes, we're almost there."

"You're Greek?"

"Yes, I'm Greek."

Once upon a time, Amalia, there was a country . . .

"Go on, Jonathan."

Once upon a time there was a family . . .

"You always told nice stories, Jonathan."

So as not to lose you, Amalia.

"Jonathan, for once, I would like to hear it from your lips."

What?

"I would like to hear your voice telling me that I . . . "

There's no chance of that happening, Amalia, forget it.

"I'm dead, Jonathan, your sister is dead. I died on Tuesday, January 8, 2013, a few days before you got your visa for your trip. I'm also at the Green-Wood Cemetery, in the well-tended grave of the Argyriou family."

It was snowing, Amalia. The park was all white that day. White and frozen. You could go ice skating on the lake. Cheep, cheep, cheep, cheep. The squirrels were freezing in their nests, cheep, cheep, cheep, cheep. Quite some time went by. Nothing.

Not a single squirrel appeared. I scattered the seeds, the acorns, the hazelnuts. Nothing. On the lake, the ducks looked like statues in a still life. Some more time went by. Cheep, cheep, cheep, cheep. Nothing. So I imitated your voice. Cheep, cheep, cheep, cheep. And then I saw him. Our little squirrel. I recognized him immediately. The tip of his tail was a little singed. It was his distinctive mark.

"*I remember, Jonathan, we named him Woody because he lived in the wood.*"

And not Woundy.

"*No more wounded names, Jonathan.*"

"Woody came running to my feet. I emptied my pockets. He sat on his hind legs and began munching on a chestnut. We remained facing each other. Frozen Jonathan and Woody with the mark on his tail. There wasn't a soul to be seen. It was ten below zero. The colorful city was protecting itself from the cold. *I want to go to Greece*, I said to myself for the first time. Woody ate one more chestnut, gave me one final glance and then ran off. January 8, 2013. Tuesday.

"Thank you for flying with Delta Air Lines. This has been our last flight to Athens. Please remain seated until the aircraft comes to a full stop."

"I died, Jonathan, your sister has died."

I never understood why.

"Don't search for answers where there are none. Beauty is an enigma, and so is suicide."

But why you, Amalia? She, Frosso Argyriou, Lale Andersen, whatever her name is, she's the one who should have . . .

"Still afraid of words, Jonathan? Repeat after me, if only this one time, say it slowly and clearly, say it so you hear it, say, 'M y   s i s t e r   d i e d.' "

Why you instead of her?

"Because no one in our family stayed in the same place till the end. We suffocate if we stay in the same place. We had our own way of loving each other, we'd switch names, roles, places, times, among ourselves."

You left me.

"I left myself. One day you look in the mirror and see a stranger's face. It's a little like a death. You want to save yourself. Even if you're going to die, you want to save yourself from that face."

"'M y   s i s t e r   d i e d.'"

"There. That's better. I took the Lexington Ave. #5 subway line downtown, I got off at City Hall, I walked across the Brooklyn Bridge. The day was breaking. For a moment I looked at the city spread

out before my eyes. The view from there, Walt Whitman had said, is 'the most effective medicine my soul has yet partaken.' I didn't need any medicine. My mind was made up. My body rose up, arched and then bent over and dove into the freezing waters of the East River. A splashing sound, and that was it. The water shifts, allowing the body to sink as much as it needs to. The river runs into the ocean."

I was left on my own.

"You were left on your own so you could make this journey."

Let me just hear the sound of your voice one more time.

"Jonathan?"

Yes, Amalia?

"I have a gift for you, Jonathan."

I'm listening.

"Close your eyes and listen to the most magical rendition of my favorite song, just listen, after all these years:

My love, I came looking for you
In the dawn and on the moon
Amid the clouds up high
I looked for you and I was blind

But then came the winter and the rain
And your grace, so fresh and cool
My love, I came looking for you
For you were made of sky . . .

*Jonathan, my voice has matured, listen to my low
notes, notice the raspiness:*

The south wind came, the north wind came
The waves will carry you off
My love you slipped away from me
For you were made of sky."[18]

Your voice. It pierces me . . .
*"Lale Andersen had a magical voice.[19] During the
War, the composer Manos Hadjidakis dreamed of
her. For her, for her voice and without ever having
met her, he wrote the song 'The North Wind Came,
the South Wind Came.' Years later, he met her and
asked her to sing it. She consented. The record went
gold. She was a foreigner. She loved Greece."*

[18] One of the earliest songs written by Manos Hadjidakis (1943).
[19] Lale Andersen was a German singer famous for her recording of
"Lili Marleen" (1939), a song which became popular among both Allied
and Axis troops.

Lale Andersen? Is that why our mother chose that name? So it would sound foreign but hide Greece inside it?

"*Nothing is what it seems, Jonathan, otherwise the world would be a very poor place.*"

The light becomes amber again. The light from the land of Menelaos, the other Frosso and Erasmia and Anthoula and Seraphim. In a sinking land, the light is not lost.

"Sir, have you filled out the form? How long are you staying in Athens?"

"How long? I really have no idea."

One's passport and identity card: paper documents that can be so easily destroyed. You only need to use your hands to tear them up into tiny little pieces. I won't do it. What existed doesn't exist anymore. But you only die when you cease to remember the ones you love. You die when your homeland shifts places on the map. It's a good land that waits for me there.

"*It's a good land that waits for you, Jonathan.*"

I get up. In the plane's toilet I change clothes. I put on a crisp white shirt. I go back to my seat and fill out the form. I hand it to the flight attendant.

"Welcome to Greece."

"Welcome to Athens, ladies and gentlemen. The weather is mild. The local time is eleven thirty, ground temperature seventeen degrees Celsius."

ABOUT THE AUTHOR

Born in Athens, Greece, Fotini Tsalikoglou studied psychology at the University of Geneva. She is the author of many celebrated novels published in Greece, including *Eros Pharmakopoios*, *I Dreamed I Was Well*, and *I, Martha Freud*. *The Secret Sister* is her English language debut.

EUROPA EDITIONS BACKLIST
(alphabetical by author)

Fiction

Carmine Abate
Between Two Seas • 978-1-933372-40-2 • Territories: World
The Homecoming Party • 978-1-933372-83-9 • Territories: World

Milena Agus
From the Land of the Moon • 978-1-60945-001-4 • Ebook • Territories:
World (excl. ANZ)

Salwa Al Neimi
The Proof of the Honey • 978-1-933372-68-6 • Ebook • Territories: World
(excl UK)

Simonetta Agnello Hornby
The Nun • 978-1-60945-062-5 • Territories: World

Daniel Arsand
Lovers • 978-1-60945-071-7 • Ebook • Territories: World

Jenn Ashworth
A Kind of Intimacy • 978-1-933372-86-0 • Territories: US & Can

Beryl Bainbridge
The Girl in the Polka Dot Dress • 978-1-60945-056-4 • Ebook •
Territories: US

Muriel Barbery
The Elegance of the Hedgehog • 978-1-933372-60-0 • Ebook • Territories:
World (excl. UK & EU)
Gourmet Rhapsody • 978-1-933372-95-2 • Ebook • Territories: World
(excl. UK & EU)

Stefano Benni
Margherita Dolce Vita • 978-1-933372-20-4 • Territories: World
Timeskipper • 978-1-933372-44-0 • Territories: World

Romano Bilenchi
The Chill • 978-1-933372-90-7 • Territories: World

Kazimierz Brandys
Rondo • 978-1-60945-004-5 • Territories: World

Alina Bronsky
Broken Glass Park • 978-1-933372-96-9 • Ebook • Territories: World
The Hottest Dishes of the Tartar Cuisine • 978-1-60945-006-9 • Ebook •
Territories: World

Jesse Browner
Everything Happens Today • 978-1-60945-051-9 • Ebook • Territories:
World (excl. UK & EU)

Francisco Coloane
Tierra del Fuego • 978-1-933372-63-1 • Ebook • Territories: World

Rebecca Connell
The Art of Losing • 978-1-933372-78-5 • Territories: US

Laurence Cossé
A Novel Bookstore • 978-1-933372-82-2 • Ebook • Territories: World
An Accident in August • 978-1-60945-049-6 • Territories: World (excl. UK)

Diego De Silva
I Hadn't Understood • 978-1-60945-065-6 • Territories: World

Shashi Deshpande
The Dark Holds No Terrors • 978-1-933372-67-9 • Territories: US

www.europaeditions.com

Steve Erickson
Zeroville • 978-1-933372-39-6 • Territories: US & Can
These Dreams of You • 978-1-60945-063-2 • Territories: US & Can

Elena Ferrante
The Days of Abandonment • 978-1-933372-00-6 • Ebook • Territories: World
Troubling Love • 978-1-933372-16-7 • Territories: World
The Lost Daughter • 978-1-933372-42-6 • Territories: World

Linda Ferri
Cecilia • 978-1-933372-87-7 • Territories: World

Damon Galgut
In a Strange Room • 978-1-60945-011-3 • Ebook • Territories: USA

Santiago Gamboa
Necropolis • 978-1-60945-073-1 • Ebook • Territories: World

Jane Gardam
Old Filth • 978-1-933372-13-6 • Ebook • Territories: US
The Queen of the Tambourine • 978-1-933372-36-5 • Ebook • Territories: US
The People on Privilege Hill • 978-1-933372-56-3 • Ebook • Territories: US
The Man in the Wooden Hat • 978-1-933372-89-1 • Ebook • Territories: US
God on the Rocks • 978-1-933372-76-1 • Ebook • Territories: US
Crusoe's Daughter • 978-1-60945-069-4 • Ebook • Territories: US

Anna Gavalda
French Leave • 978-1-60945-005-2 • Ebook • Territories: US & Can

Seth Greenland
The Angry Buddhist • 978-1-60945-068-7 • Ebook • Territories: World

Katharina Hacker
The Have-Nots • 978-1-933372-41-9 • Territories: World (excl. India)

Patrick Hamilton
Hangover Square • 978-1-933372-06-8 • Territories: US & Can

James Hamilton-Paterson
Cooking with Fernet Branca • 978-1-933372-01-3 • Territories: US
Amazing Disgrace • 978-1-933372-19-8 • Territories: US
Rancid Pansies • 978-1-933372-62-4 • Territories: USA

Alfred Hayes
The Girl on the Via Flaminia • 978-1-933372-24-2 • Ebook •
Territories: World

Jean-Claude Izzo
The Lost Sailors • 978-1-933372-35-8 • Territories: World
A Sun for the Dying • 978-1-933372-59-4 • Territories: World

Gail Jones
Sorry • 978-1-933372-55-6 • Territories: US & Can

Ioanna Karystiani
The Jasmine Isle • 978-1-933372-10-5 • Territories: World
Swell • 978-1-933372-98-3 • Territories: World

Peter Kocan
Fresh Fields • 978-1-933372-29-7 • Territories: US, EU & Can
The Treatment and the Cure • 978-1-933372-45-7 • Territories: US, EU & Can

Helmut Krausser
Eros • 978-1-933372-58-7 • Territories: World

Amara Lakhous
Clash of Civilizations Over an Elevator in Piazza Vittorio •
978-1-933372-61-7 • Ebook • Territories: World
Divorce Islamic Style • 978-1-60945-066-3 • Ebook • Territories: World

Lia Levi
The Jewish Husband • 978-1-933372-93-8 • Territories: World

Valerio Massimo Manfredi
The Ides of March • 978-1-933372-99-0 • Territories: US

Leïla Marouane
The Sexual Life of an Islamist in Paris • 978-1-933372-85-3 •
Territories: World

Lorenzo Mediano
The Frost on His Shoulders • 978-1-60945-072-4 • Ebook •
Territories: World

Sélim Nassib
I Loved You for Your Voice • 978-1-933372-07-5 • Territories: World
The Palestinian Lover • 978-1-933372-23-5 • Territories: World

Amélie Nothomb
Tokyo Fiancée • 978-1-933372-64-8 • Territories: US & Can
Hygiene and the Assassin • 978-1-933372-77-8 • Ebook • Territories: US & Can

Valeria Parrella
For Grace Received • 978-1-933372-94-5 • Territories: World

Alessandro Piperno
The Worst Intentions • 978-1-933372-33-4 • Territories: World
Persecution • 978-1-60945-074-8 • Ebook • Territories: World

Lorcan Roche
The Companion • 978-1-933372-84-6 • Territories: World

Boualem Sansal
The German Mujahid • 978-1-933372-92-1 • Ebook • Territories: US & Can

www.europaeditions.com

Eric-Emmanuel Schmitt
The Most Beautiful Book in the World • 978-1-933372-74-7 • Ebook •
Territories: World
The Woman with the Bouquet • 978-1-933372-81-5 • Ebook • Territories:
US & Can

Angelika Schrobsdorff
You Are Not Like Other Mothers • 978-1-60945-075-5 • Ebook •
Territories: World

Audrey Schulman
Three Weeks in December • 978-1-60945-064-9 • Ebook • Territories: US
& Can

James Scudamore
Heliopolis • 978-1-933372-73-0 • Ebook • Territories: US

Luis Sepúlveda
The Shadow of What We Were • 978-1-60945-002-1 • Ebook • Territories:
World

Paolo Sorrentino
Everybody's Right • 978-1-60945-052-6 • Ebook • Territories: US & Can

Domenico Starnone
First Execution • 978-1-933372-66-2 • Territories: World

Henry Sutton
Get Me out of Here • 978-1-60945-007-6 • Ebook • Territories: US & Can

Chad Taylor
Departure Lounge • 978-1-933372-09-9 • Territories: US, EU & Can

Roma Tearne
Mosquito • 978-1-933372-57-0 • Territories: US & Can
Bone China • 978-1-933372-75-4 • Territories: US

André Carl van der Merwe
Moffie • 978-1-60945-050-2 • Ebook • Territories: World
(excl. S. Africa)

Fay Weldon
Chalcot Crescent • 978-1-933372-79-2 • Territories: US

Anne Wiazemsky
My Berlin Child • 978-1-60945-003-8 • Territories: US & Can

Jonathan Yardley
Second Reading • 978-1-60945-008-3 • Ebook • Territories: US & Can

Edwin M. Yoder Jr.
Lions at Lamb House • 978-1-933372-34-1 • Territories: World

Michele Zackheim
Broken Colors • 978-1-933372-37-2 • Territories: World

Alice Zeniter
Take This Man • 978-1-60945-053-3 • Territories: World

Tonga Books

Ian Holding
Of Beasts and Beings • 978-1-60945-054-0 • Ebook • Territories: US & Can

Sara Levine
Treasure Island!!! • 978-0-14043-768-3 • Ebook • Territories: World

Alexander Maksik
You Deserve Nothing • 978-1-60945-048-9 • Ebook • Territories: US, Can & EU (excl. UK)

Thad Ziolkowski
Wichita • 978-1-60945-070-0 • Ebook • Territories: World

Crime/Noir

Massimo Carlotto
The Goodbye Kiss • 978-1-933372-05-1 • Ebook • Territories: World
Death's Dark Abyss • 978-1-933372-18-1 • Ebook • Territories: World
The Fugitive • 978-1-933372-25-9 • Ebook • Territories: World
Bandit Love • 978-1-933372-80-8 • Ebook • Territories: World
Poisonville • 978-1-933372-91-4 • Ebook • Territories: World

Giancarlo De Cataldo
The Father and the Foreigner • 978-1-933372-72-3 • Territories: World

Caryl Férey
Zulu • 978-1-933372-88-4 • Ebook • Territories: World (excl. UK & EU)
Utu • 978-1-60945-055-7 • Ebook • Territories: World (excl. UK & EU)

Alicia Giménez-Bartlett
Dog Day • 978-1-933372-14-3 • Territories: US & Can
Prime Time Suspect • 978-1-933372-31-0 • Territories: US & Can
Death Rites • 978-1-933372-54-9 • Territories: US & Can

Jean-Claude Izzo
Total Chaos • 978-1-933372-04-4 • Territories: US & Can
Chourmo • 978-1-933372-17-4 • Territories: US & Can
Solea • 978-1-933372-30-3 • Territories: US & Can

www.europaeditions.com

Matthew F. Jones
Boot Tracks • 978-1-933372-11-2 • Territories: US & Can

Gene Kerrigan
The Midnight Choir • 978-1-933372-26-6 • Territories: US & Can
Little Criminals • 978-1-933372-43-3 • Territories: US & Can

Carlo Lucarelli
Carte Blanche • 978-1-933372-15-0 • Territories: World
The Damned Season • 978-1-933372-27-3 • Territories: World
Via delle Oche • 978-1-933372-53-2 • Territories: World

Edna Mazya
Love Burns • 978-1-933372-08-2 • Territories: World (excl. ANZ)

Yishai Sarid
Limassol • 978-1-60945-000-7 • Ebook • Territories: World (excl. UK, AUS & India)

Joel Stone
The Jerusalem File • 978-1-933372-65-5 • Ebook • Territories: World

Benjamin Tammuz
Minotaur • 978-1-933372-02-0 • Ebook • Territories: World

Non-fiction

Alberto Angela
A Day in the Life of Ancient Rome • 978-1-933372-71-6 • Territories: World • History

Helmut Dubiel
Deep In the Brain: Living with Parkinson's Disease • 978-1-933372-70-9 •
Ebook • Territories: World • Medicine/Memoir

James Hamilton-Paterson
Seven-Tenths: The Sea and Its Thresholds • 978-1-933372-69-3 • Territories:
USA • Nature/Essays

Daniele Mastrogiacomo
Days of Fear • 978-1-933372-97-6 • Ebook • Territories: World • Current
affairs/Memoir/Afghanistan/Journalism

Valery Panyushkin
Twelve Who Don't Agree • 978-1-60945-010-6 • Ebook • Territories:
World • Current affairs/Memoir/Russia/Journalism

Christa Wolf
One Day a Year: 1960-2000 • 978-1-933372-22-8 • Territories: World •
Memoir/History/20th Century

Children's Illustrated Fiction

Altan
Here Comes Timpa • 978-1-933372-28-0 • Territories: World (excl. Italy)
Timpa Goes to the Sea • 978-1-933372-32-7 • Territories: World (excl. Italy)
Fairy Tale Timpa • 978-1-933372-38-9 • Territories: World (excl. Italy)

Wolf Erlbruch
The Big Question • 978-1-933372-03-7 • Territories: US & Can
The Miracle of the Bears • 978-1-933372-21-1 • Territories: US & Can
(with **Gioconda Belli**) *The Butterfly Workshop* • 978-1-933372-12-9 •
Territories: US & Can